Copyright@ 2022 K. T. Seto
Parallel: A Collection of Science Fiction Short Stories
The Ark © 2021 K.T. Seto, Vocal. Media—Fiction.
Species 24 © 2021 K.T. Seto, Vocal. Media—Fiction.
Red House © 2022 K.T. Seto, Vocal. Media—Fiction.
Reset © 2021 K.T. Seto, Vocal. Media—Fiction.
Apoptosis© 2020 K.T. Seto, Nightmare Whispers Vol 3
Cake © 2021 K.T. Seto, Vocal. Media—Fiction.
Come Play With Me © 2021 K.T. Seto, Vocal. Media—Fiction.
Labme #7 © 2021 K.T. Seto, Vocal. Media—Fiction.
Moon Bull © 2021 K.T. Seto, Vocal. Media—Fiction.
Spin © 2021 K.T. Seto, Vocal. Media—Fiction.
Safe © 2021 K.T. Seto, Vocal. Media—Fiction.
The Call © 2021 K.T. Seto, Vocal. Media—Fiction.
Sanitation 6 © 2022 K.T. Seto, Parallel
Just Don't Look © 2022 K.T. Seto, Parallel
Moving On © 2022 K.T. Seto, Parallel
A Bucket of Hope © 2022 K.T. Seto, Parallel
Zeroed Out © 2022 K.T. Seto, Teman Cooke, Parallel
Trues © 2021 K.T. Seto, Vocal. Media—Fiction.
The Job© 2020 K.T. Seto, Fractured Realities
Enhanced © 2022 K.T. Seto, Vocal. Media—Fiction.

This is a work of fiction. Names, characters, places, and incidents either are the product of the author's imagination or are used fictitiously. Any resemblance to actual persons, living or dead, events, or locales is entirely coincidental.

All rights reserved. No part of this publication may be reproduced, distributed, or transmitted in any form by any means, including photocopying, recording, or other electronic methods without the prior written permission of the author, except in the case of brief quotations embodied in reviews and certain other noncommercial uses permitted by copyright law. For permission requests, write to the author at the address below.
katsetowriter@gmail.com
ISBN: 9781087882024

Parallel: A Collection Of Science Fiction Short Stories

PARALLEL: ANTHOLOGY OF SHORT STORIES

A Collection of Science Fiction Short Stories

K.T. SETO

Parallel: A Collection Of Science Fiction Short Stories

Table of Contents

PART ONE............................ 4
   ODDITIES........................ 4
2................................... 6
   The Ark......................... 6
3................................... 16
   Red House....................... 16
4................................... 32
   Reset........................... 32
5................................... 40
   Apoptosis....................... 40
IMAGININGS.......................... 51
7................................... 53
   Cake............................ 53
8................................... 57
   Come Play With Me............... 57
9................................... 62
   Labme #7........................ 62
10.................................. 71
   Moon Bull....................... 71
11.................................. 77
   Spin............................ 77
12.................................. 83
   Safe............................ 83

Parallel: A Collection Of Science Fiction Short Stories

```
13.................................. 90
   The Call...................... 90
ENVISIONINGS...................... 97
15.................................100
   Sanitation 6...................100
16.................................120
   Just Don't Look................120
      I...........................120
      II..........................142
17.................................158
   Moving On.....................158
18.................................167
   A Bucket of Hope...............167
19.................................193
   Zeroed Out.....................193
20.................................225
   Trues..........................225
21.................................231
   The Job........................231
22.................................256
   Enhanced.......................256
```

Parallel: A Collection Of Science Fiction Short Stories

PART ONE

ODDITIES

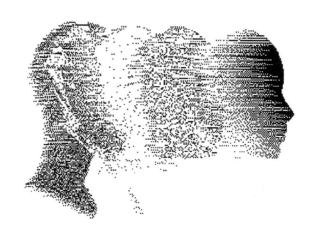

Parallel: A Collection Of Science Fiction Short Stories

As a Speculative Fiction writer in the 21st century, you have to be willing to take risks and do it all. Which means you have to get very comfortable with the marketing side of things. Most writers take that as explicit instructions to write a blog. While I did eventually try my hand at this, I remain skeptical as to its use or value as, ultimately; I am a storyteller not a reporter. I love to write stories. To build a following, I started writing short stories and putting them up for free on a site I found that is perfect for that. It is a way to play with ideas that might or might not work in longer form. The original intention of my works on the VM site was to free myself of expectations and just create hoping someone will enjoy. All the stories in part one are bits that don't fit. Odd tales of 'what if?' I initially published the first four on the VM site. The last one, "Apoptosis", appeared originally in a horror anthology called *Nightmare Whispers*. I readily admit sometimes my imagination is quite disturbing and rather off. Which I feel is the perfect reason to inflict it upon the general population. Why should my friends be the only ones who get to be confused and disturbed by me?

2
The Ark

Utopia isn't a place, really. It's an idea. Or, better yet, an ideal to seek. It's ubiquitous because it pops up in many ways throughout history and in myths and legends. Through the ages we have always had stories that allude to some great perfect moment coming. The dream of it is alluring. As a child, I always hoped it could happen. I read the classics and watched the old speculative fiction movie streams from a young age. The ones where humans imagined what the world would look like in a future without all of life's petty problems. Where everyone had come together as a species and made great things happen. Nothing I read or saw ever convinced me that such a place, such an ideal, could exist. Because I knew people. The people around me and the history of our countries with their selfishness and wars. People, even when they have everything they could ever hope to have or wish for, never seemed to settle down and have that moment. Something spoils it, looms on the horizon, or festers underneath. Yet, some part of me still hopes despite the constant stream of evidence proving that Utopia is impossible. Which makes this meeting even more tragic, because we have solved so many problems but not the most basic— human nature. The light in the conference room hurt my eyes, but I didn't dare look away from the table for even an instant. Too many of the dignitaries gathered there would take even an extra blink as a sign of something. What, I didn't know. I could barely keep up with the intrigue in the room and the petty games politicians still played, even in this enlightened age. There were three dozen of us in the room, seated in amazingly comfortable chairs around the large round table. The gleaming surface of it resembled the ancient hand-carved Scandinavian woodwork of the late 20th century. Of course, it wasn't wood. No one has used something so precious for furnishings in over a hundred years. They'd grouped us by position rather than by region, which is why I and the other scientists called upon to testify sat together. It meant I knew the people sitting on either side of me. Doctor Ito Akari, a cytogeneticist from New Tokyo, sat on my right, her eyes moving around the room and back to her table display where a series of formulas shifted and flowed in a manner that told me she was still working on the problem even as the politicians sat before us pondering solutions. On my left sat Doctor Yonas Gebremariam, climatologist from Kasai, one of the two remaining countries in West Africa. He watched the room with heavy-lidded eyes that to the unschooled might seem inattentive. Yet I have known Yonas for over twenty years and there was no one who could sum up a room in a glance the way he could.

"The people on the Utopia Project chose to leave; I don't think there is any need for discussion here," a fair-haired man said from the end of the table. I couldn't see his ID badge from where I sat and didn't bother queuing it up on my table display. If he was important I would already know his name, though he looked vaguely familiar.

"Are you actually suggesting we leave them to their fates?" the man next to him said, and I leaned forward a bit, the urge to rub my eyes becoming unbearable. This one I knew just by the sound of his voice: Pieter Dragovich, the ambassador from the Siberian Block. They hadn't bothered to send their president, their country's stance on the issue being well-known. It was doubtful that anything said here today would change it.

"Isn't that what they did to us?" the fair-haired one said waspishly in reply. No one answered him. In all honesty, he'd said what we'd all been thinking. Deep down we all felt like they deserved it. Let them rot, the small, mean part of me said. They didn't care about us; about anything. Guilt assailed me for the thought, so I cleared my throat in preparation to speak to the room at large. After all, they'd made me spokesperson. Drawing straws, an archaic and egalitarian method of choosing the sacrificial lamb to toss to the wolves so to speak.

"That is not who we are, not who we have become as a people. Where is the compassion and integrity you all preach?" I said, pushing down that tiny bit of resentment.

"Don't toss out platitudes and campaign slogans, Doctor King. We are talking about an entire ship full of the worst parts of humanity. Every person living there was so firmly entrenched in the past that they chose to flee rather than stay and make the hard choices necessary to save our species."

"I know what and who they are." I didn't raise my voice but couldn't entirely keep the anger from my tone.

"We asked Doctor King and the others here in an advisory capacity. We don't need emotion or opinions, we need facts. If no one has an objection, why don't we revise the order of our schedule and allow Doctor King to provide the findings of his team before continuing this discussion."

I turned to look at the British Prime Minister and gave her a nod of recognition for her support. Her knack for diffusing difficult situations was why she'd remained in power for so long.

"Very well," I said looking back at the man who'd first spoken. I pulled up his name on my display, dismayed to find that I couldn't dismiss him out of hand.

"Mr. Vice President, you are correct; their ancestors did choose to leave, but *they* didn't.

The Ark has been in orbit longer than most of them have been alive. Maintained and updated by AI that gives them a filtered stream of information about what is going on here on the surface. We have never once offered any of them the chance to make a different choice. From their orbit above the Earth, they can see the changes we have wrought in their absence. They are not completely isolated. They know the world is not the same one their great-grandparents left." I ran my gaze around the room before continuing.

"However, all of this is moot. The fact is, they have lived too long in space to return. We have run all the numbers and projections. They could not stand full gravity. It would kill them all within weeks. Their request for resettlement is not possible. Our only option is to offer them help with repairs."

The silence that filled the room after my statement didn't surprise me. I, and the other five scientists who'd led the teams — studying this problem since the Ark sent out the SOS six months ago — had known our findings would cause issues.

"If their own AI can't repair things, what's to say anything we have will be any more effective?" The Chinese Prime Minister's voice was soft but carried around the room despite the lack of amplification. I looked at her and suppressed the urge to sigh. Did no one read the reports given to them?

"What they need is attainable with our current technology. Theirs is still several decades behind." Doctor Ito interjected without taking her eyes off her display. It was clear something there worried her, and I wished I had a moment to confer before dealing with more bureaucracy.

"How is that even possible? Mandatory updates being what they are." I looked over at the American Vice President again, stifling the urge to snap at him. Reading in the 23rd century was apparently not common among the ruling class.

"The creators of the Ark intended their system to be self-sustaining to better withstand intrusions by hackers and any other outside forces. They didn't want us to be able to sabotage them."

"Why would anyone left behind sabotage them? They sought to escape the destruction of their own making. They designed their

Ark station to provide a new world to replace the one they'd destroyed." There were several smothered laughs around the room in response to this statement. I waited a beat then continued.

"We can send a ship and supplies to them and make the repairs. It will save their lives, and the Ark will be able to remain in orbit for another fifty years."

"So, their refuge is to be their prison?" PM Sussex asked, and the Vice President made a low sound I chose to ignore before replying.

"This was a choice their ancestors made, not a punishment for their crimes. It is not as if they lack for anything. They spared no expense in the creation of the Ark, the equivalent of hundreds of trillions of dollars," I said, pulling up the specifications of the Ark and instructing the computer to display them on everyone's tablets.

"It is wealth they could have used to fix this planet in a few years rather than decades. They chose to leave. It was the height of selfishness, and truly short-sighted. Some might say that they should go to prison for what they did. I am not among that group. It is only human nature to be concerned with personal well-being. And those who committed the crimes are long gone," Yonas said, and I saw several people jump in surprise. Clearly some had thought him sleeping. I suppressed a smile and pulled up the next slide.

"You said fifty years? Then what?" a voice from the back of the room asked, and I turned to face the speaker even though they were too far for me to see.

"We have fifty years to develop a means for them to either return to Earth or abandon them to their fates."

"So, we fix the ship and kick the problem down the road to our successors," the voice replied, and I shrugged.

"You asked us to find an immediate solution. This is the best we can do."

The meeting ended after another hour of pontificating and disagreements that changed nothing. My testimony had negated the need to decide much more than who would deliver the news. I remained seated as the important people began to leave, watching Doctor Ito scan her display and shake her head.

"You didn't add anything," I said quietly.

"Because they'd never go for it. I have no patience for politics, you know this."

"But you have something," I pressed, and she nodded.

"It's not ideal." I waited and she leaned close, looking over her shoulder to keep others from listening in.

"The children. If we brought them back, we could potentially reintegrate them."

"But not the adults," I said quietly.

"No one who has hit puberty." We exchanged a look and then I nodded.

"Better not to tell them."

3
Red House

"A candle is burning in the window of the abandoned cabin. You know, the one in the woods?" The statement echoed in my ears. I couldn't speak for a full minute. My throat just closed up.

"You know we're not supposed to go in there, right?" I asked when I could speak again, and Evan nodded. "Do you know why?" He shrugged but didn't answer. He couldn't understand my reaction, I guess. He'd said a candle burned in the window and I'd dropped my mug, spilling my half-caf all over. Because every word in his statement scared me. Like it scares me every time I think about what happened. Starting with the woods. They were the second reason they'd abandoned the cabin. Well, abandoned it here. The great red forest.

Parallel: A Collection Of Science Fiction Short Stories

In the beginning, terraforming Mars was an idea that appealed to everyone, but creating trees and other vegetation that survived and thrived in the domed surface colonies required a level of genetic manipulation and investment that governments seldom want to sustain for long. So they left the vegetation to its own devices, and the woods had evolved into something only vaguely related to their Earth-native counterparts. Every so often, someone else swept in and tried to tame things, but they always gave up.

The NAA—North American Alliance—started this. It had been their idea to model the new forest after Yellowstone—the first of the fully restored national parks on Earth. They'd done a full study of which plants could survive here, then arranged everything according to their plan. Unfortunately, the latter part of their plan included installing the cabin. The main reason they'd abandoned everything.

They'd wanted an authentic forest ranger cabin. If they could have put a bowtie-wearing bear in there, too, they'd have been happy. Someone located an abandoned cabin they considered authentic enough and in good enough shape to disassemble, transport and reassemble, and stuck it in the middle of their newly planted vegetation, furnishing it with high-quality reproductions of early 19th-century pieces. Perched as it was amid the rust-colored trees and spindly foliage, it loomed in a way that put the final nail in the coffin of the project. It never looked remotely welcoming. Not at all. The combination of the two made certain that no one would ever want to go into the new forest again. Much like the surrounding forest, they had left the cabin to its own devices for far too long. The structure was intact, but the appearance had fallen victim to neglect; both on Mars and back on Earth. They'd repaired the windows, but it hadn't mattered. No one who entered the cabin ever wanted to set foot in it again. And after last time, they'd told us to keep out officially.

"I suppose I should tell you what happened. You know, the other time it was lit so you understand," I said, and he shrugged. I closed my eyes and nodded, resigning myself to revisit the nightmare, on purpose this time, because the candle was lit. Understanding is part of the ritual, part of what has to happen.

"You know how the cabin got here, right? How the government brought it over with the first permanent settlers? How they worked to get it right, down to the smallest details. Like the candle. It's a fat, hand-molded column of paraffin created using the ancient modeling methods. It sits in a replica lantern on the window ledge as part of the art installation with the painting of the lost ranger. Until that night, no one had ever lit it. Or even thought it could be lit. But like everything commissioned as part of the project, the artist contracted to recreate the ancient device had worked for authenticity, so it was a real candle in a real lantern. Or as close as anything on the Red Planet can come." I looked at the poor kid whose job it was to make sure no one trespassed in the forest at night. It was fifteen minutes after midnight. With a start, I realized it was around the same time we'd seen the candle the night it happened. We use the same clock on Mars, but our hours are longer to help better sync our time to the home-world. He was humoring me. I could tell he couldn't care less about anything other than if he would get in trouble because someone had gone in after dark and messed with things.

"It was a night like tonight, around midnight. The candle was lit so the kid on patrol duty, his name was Willard, came here to tell the MOD. The two of them called me and I agreed to meet them there." I shook my head. "You know how the forest is at night. It gets funny. The things that live there, GM mammals, birds that escaped the aviary, and the muggies, all come out to play. The noises they make are enough to make your blood run cold. They assigned me a patrol on the other edge of the forest. You know Gamma quadrant, so I couldn't see or hear anything until I got closer. When I did, I heard the muggies hum." I swallowed and skewed my face.

"That's what that is? I heard the humming, but I couldn't tell what was making the noise or where it was coming from. Kind of creeped me out the way it seemed to come from everywhere and nowhere," Evan said, sliding into the chair on the other side of my desk. He kept looking down at my spilled drink and broken cup, but I continued to ignore it. It wasn't important.

"It's because of the Buhag, but I'm getting ahead of myself. See, we all knew about the painting. The painting starts it. They light the candle, then the painting goes blank and the muggies sing to welcome him back." I wiped a hand over my face. "The guy who sold them the cabin gave them the painting, too. Said they went together and would make it more authentic. I looked him up later. He hanged himself six months after the sale. He left a letter, saying it came back. Said it wanted to take him for a ride. No one knew what that meant."

"You're making this sound all melodramatic. Get to the point. This is the 22nd century, man. No one believes in monsters and fairytales anymore." The kid blinked rapidly as he said this. I stared at him and nodded at his statement before waving it off.

"True. But don't you wonder why those kinds of tales persist? Even with our advances in science and technology? Because every story has a grain of truth. Like the story about the lost ranger. He really existed." Evan blinked again and nodded carefully. I stood, motioning for him to follow me.

"Come on, we'd better go see if it's still burning. I'll tell you the rest as we go." I picked up my kit and tightened my holster, making sure I had everything I needed. Evan silently followed me outside, then came up beside me so he could hear me talk. The night air was close and humid, typical for the dome, and the ground was slightly spongy as if the Red Planet didn't know what to do with all the moisture after being dry for so long.

"That night, I made a wide circle around the outside of the forest so I could complete my circuit and still meet up with them near the main entrance. The humming got louder the closer I got to the area they'd told me to meet them in. It had a kind of rhythm. A low buzz/hum that repeated like a beacon or a drum. But it wasn't a sound made by anything man made. I saw clusters of muggies in the grass."

"They're everywhere tonight," Evan agreed, and pushed one of the six-legged insects out of the way with his foot. No one stepped on muggies. Besides being a protected species, as the first naturally evolved insect in Mars colony, if you crushed their hard exoskeletons their insides let off a smell that brought tears to your eyes whilst simultaneously making you sick to your stomach. And it lasted for days. Something the early colonists discovered the hard way.

"When I got to where they'd told me to meet them, no one was around. I saw something moving in the shadows and turned on my torch so I could peer inside the tree line. A trio of capybaras was just inside the forest. Their dark red fur was slicked around their face and much darker, as if they'd dipped them into slime or mud. When I turned the light on them, they hissed and ran away. Not unusual, but it added to my growing trepidation. Looking down, I saw footprints leading into the forest. I'd thought the MOD and Willard had made them, so I followed them." I pulled out my flashlight and turned it on, shining it on the ground and then over Evan, who blinked at the light and moved a couple of steps away so he was out of the beam.

"You make those?" I asked, shining my light on the footprints in the soft dirt leading into the forest.

"What? No. I came from the other direction, east of here, and left the same way.

Well, a little closer, but still not here. Not on this path."

I lifted the flashlight, angling the shaft of light deeper into the trees. The line of footprints was clear. Then I looked at Evan and nodded, motioning for him to follow.

"The deeper I went into the forest, the louder the buzz/hum became. It creeped me out. Creeped me out more, that is. I remembered what they'd said about the lost ranger." I trudged on. The only light was the small shaft from my flashlight. The woods were thick, too thick for any light to penetrate this deep into the forest at night. Once we got to the clearing that held the cabin, we'd be able to see the moons again, and the candle if it was still lit.

"Careful, you don't want to step on a muggie. You should walk closer to me, so you have more light," I said, looking over my shoulder at Evan. He nodded but didn't close the gap.

"What did they say about the lost ranger? How did he get lost?" Evan asked, and I slowed my steps, in no hurry to reach the cabin.

"It was around 400 or 500 years ago. Had to be a long time, these things are weak at first. He wasn't a ranger, but a trapper. Part of a dying breed, as factories were just invented and edging out the mom-and-pop operations as the industrial age got rolling. He'd built the cabin for his wife and hunted game in the forest and fished in the lake that was nearby. Every day she'd light a candle and set it in the window in case he came home after dark. A regiment of soldiers on their way to someplace called Texas Territory was passing through the forest and came upon the cabin." I looked back at Evan. He was breathing heavily, even though I'd slowed my pace. "They broke in and had their way with the wife. Her husband walked in on them near the end. He killed a couple outright, and two more while trying to get his wife away, but it was too late. She was too far gone. She died in his arms. Then they chased him into the woods. Every time they caught up they'd cut him. At first he moved quickly, but as the night wore on he slowed until he was walking, then crawling. They left his body in the woods." I turned to look at Evan, shining the light on him and then down at the ground again. He was moving slower now, almost stumbling along behind me. I sighed and picked up the tale.

"Ten years later, someone found the cabin. Started living there but left because of all the weirdness. They'd come home and their lantern would be lit. They'd hear a man's voice shouting at them to leave. Or they'd hear someone following them in the woods. Over the years others would try to live there, but they'd all leave, until finally they found an old doctor of some sort who told them that the lost man had become a Buhag." I didn't turn around when I said it. We were almost to the clearing and I could see the candle was indeed still lit.

"What's a Buhag?" Evan rasped. I spared a quick glance over my shoulder, wondering if I would have time to finish the tale. Not that I needed to wonder, I knew the way of things and how it had to go. There would be time, only as much as needed.

"Some people believe that folks who die through violence and are left unburied come back as evil spirits. Monsters, if you will, the kind that suck the life from your body and take your skin so they can have flesh again. For a little while," I said, walking into the clearing and standing to wait for Evan to join me.

"You don't believe that, do you?"

"I have to. Because that night, the night the candle was lit, the muggies called and he came. He came and took Willard for a ride. Then he tried to take Bain, the MOD. But he passed out from fright and then ran back to the station while I was still walking out towards the cabin. They have to be awake for it to take them. Awake and unaware." Evan got to the clearing and blinked rapidly at the change in lighting. The moons of Mars shone their dull reflection of the sun's light in the clearing, casting wavy shadows all around. In the cabin's window the candle's flame danced merrily, and I knew if I was dumb enough to go inside the painting, that damn painting, would be blank.

"What happened?" Evan asked, and I shook my head.

"You know. It's time to come out now. Go blow out the candle and let Evan rest."

"What are you saying?" Evan said, and took a step backward. I turned and took a step towards the cabin.

"Or I can go burn the painting and set the place on fire. I have everything I need to do it right here. You should let me do it. Then you'll be free." I reached slowly into my holster and pulled out my pistol, holding it by my side.

"You're talking crazy. Don't go in there. You can see the candle is burning. We need to search the woods to see if we can find who lit it."

"So we can get lost? That's what you want, right? Company? Revenge? That's why you tricked him into lighting the candle. That's why you came to tell me about it. It didn't work then, and it won't work now. Come out," I said, bracing myself.

"You're talking crazy. We should go. You know what? We don't need to search, I don't care who lit it. You're scaring me."

"You've said that before. No one can see the candle from outside of the forest, Evan. Go inside. Blow out the candle, let him rest. You remember what happened last time? How we fought, how you tried to take me and failed because I wasn't unaware and guarded myself against you? Do you remember how you pulled off Willard's skin and tried to strangle me with it?" I said in a low voice, and Evan shook his head, his breathing picking up again as if he was gearing up to do something hard.

"I just want..." Evan began, and I lifted the pistol and shot him in his right shoulder so he could see I meant what I was saying.

"There's a third way. Do you remember what happened that night? Evan won't, he wasn't there. But then again, he's not here either, is he?" I pulled the trigger again and shot him in his other shoulder. Like the first time, he didn't cry out, just shielded his eyes from the light of the pistol's focused laser beam.

"I'll go, I just want..." Evan began, then his face contorted and he lunged at me. I fell backwards to evade him and lost my balance, falling to the spongy ground, then rolled and leaped to my feet, putting several feet between us as not-Evan took several clumsy steps in my direction, arms outstretched. That's when the smell hit me. The smell of blood, the smell of decay lingering in the night air and making my heart race. I dodged his grasping hands and feinted towards him, circling and moving so he moved closer and closer to the cabin. He just needed to be on the step.

"I beat you before. I beat you before," I chanted as he caught a hold of me and we struggled. Even though I knew it was coming it still sickened me as Evan's flesh peeled away, leaving bloody bones behind. "Off me! Off me! Off me!" I grunted, slipping out from its grasp and rolling toward the steps. *Can't touch them. Has to be him*, I thought and jumped away again as not-Evan lunged for me and missed, flailing, and stumbled backward onto the bottom step of the cabin's porch. It was the moment I was waiting for. I raised the pistol again and shot him in the chest. The force of it knocked him down and he crawled backward, trying to regain his feet, towards the door of the cabin. I shot out his knee and he let out what sounded like a cry before standing and stumbling back into the open doorway. He stood there swaying, blood and ichor dripping from his wounds and the places where his skin had peeled away. It wasn't a sight I would forget soon, if ever. I clamped my lips together, let him see the resolution in my eyes. Let him see it coming. He was used to that after all, had to have been after all this time.

"Ride is over, mister. That kid should have had a long life," I said bitterly, as I carefully aimed and fired one last blast from my laser pistol at the spot between not-Evan's eyes. The shot knocked him backward into the doorway of the cabin.

And the candle went out.

4

Reset

We were six clicks out from civilian compound 23 when my sensors picked up a pod. I had a split second to alert my team then I dived behind the nearest pile of rubble and pressed the heel of my hand to my locket for luck. It had yet to fail me and didn't this time. The explosion delivered the viral payload in a tight circle around the trigger, stopping inches short of the pile I hid behind. The second Geneva Convention outlawed use of bio-gens in warfare but the off-worlders never signed anything, did they? After all, they didn't want to hurt the planet. They just wanted us gone. Sometimes I wondered if they were right. It's not like we weren't guilty of what they were punishing us for.

I was six when the off-worlders arrived, living with my mother in what was left of the East Coast of the USA at the end of the last Human War. Rebuilding had barely begun, and the governments of the world were still meeting to squabble over what would and wouldn't be allowed in the future, trying to pave a path out of extremism and destruction. Then the ships arrived. I remember standing outside, holding my mother's hand, looking up at the sky. Feeling the awe and fear that comes with having big questions answered and finding the answers more than you want to accept. I remember listening to the news streams about our attempts to communicate, to let them know we are intelligent and this planet is inhabited. The frantic attempts to convince the un-convincible that we mattered. And failing. It was understandable really; how could they tell the difference between us and a dangerous parasitic organism? We remade our host to suit our needs and sapped the life from it to grow stronger. The planet is what mattered you see. Integral to the galactic ecosystem. We disturbed the balance.

My helmet muffled the sound of the pod's explosion and the screams of the two team members caught in the path of the blast. I was glad. The initial reaction to the virus was painful in the extreme. I had seen people pull out a gun and end it rather than suffer. My hands shook a bit as I crouched, waiting to see if they would come. Some pods needed tending. The tended, that's what we call the poor souls relegated to that horrid in between place. The one that sits between humanity and the inanimate, a living barometer used for measuring the effects of the changes to the area around it. Plant herders, we call it purgatory. No one used to know what that looks like. Those were the ones we steered clear of. We hadn't at first. The ego of humanity. At first, we'd tried to ambush and destroy. But human stubbornness and the drive to conquer had met the brick wall of off-world will. We soon came to accept our new reality. Mere pebbles in the path of the waves. We might survive, but not as we were. Not before being broken down and swept out into the path determined by the strength of the water washing over us.

    Only the sound of my teammates' cries lingered in the air, but still we waited. Our only assurance of safety now was stealth. Corralled as we were into compounds and underground shelters, we'd learned not to venture far from our assigned spaces with great pain and heavy losses. I wanted to move so I stifled the urge by pulling out my locket and wrapping my hand around it, so the slight weight pressed into the creases of my hand. I remembered when my mother passed it to me. This small silver locket. My great-grandfather had given it to my great-grandmother as a present. I didn't remember them; they'd died when I was three, in the first wave of destruction that commenced in the mercifully short last Human War. They'd called it World War III at first, until they'd realized that was the last time humanity would ever fight each other.

There was unity in death. Death was a moment when the living things around it paused to acknowledge the transition and meaningfulness of existence. Faced with causing death on a large scale, humans united to try to explain and prevent it in the future. Faced with annihilation from an outside superior force, humanity united to preserve our species as a whole. The off-worlders did the impossible. They taught humans to look past selfishness and petty distinctions and stand together.

My team lead gave the 'all clear' in my headset and I stood, reluctant to leave my shelter but knowing I had a duty to my fallen comrades, their screams little more than low moans as the virus took hold and began to cut off anything resembling human like speech. All of the remaining team members, the six of us untouched by the pod's effects, gathered in a tight circle around the two lying on the ground. Odd how humans would always seek to make a ritual out of everything. I supposed it gave us meaning and helped us deal with the things that taxed our emotions and capacity for understanding. The lead nodded, and we sank to the ground, getting as comfortable as we could for the wait. Sometimes it took a long time, depending on what they'd decided the area needed. Seldom was it quick and merciful, but that was the one truth in life, the brutality of change. Change was painful, no matter the type.

I rocked a bit where I sat, my hand clasped around my locket as I murmured the words we all learned prior to assignment in the field.

"From the Earth we come, to the Earth we return. The life we have will take new form. Not

ending but beginning anew, we honor and remember you." I chanted it three times then forced myself to look. Jy and Raz. Sighing, I shook my head. I'd liked them. Always a joke or a kind word. They'd been in the field longer than anyone else I knew and kept the team's spirits up even amidst the fear. They weren't human now.

The pods disintegrated chemical bonds in seconds. Simple bonds, like those in clothing, went immediately. Then the more complex. Teeth, hair, skin, bones. Everything infected and remade in moments. The telltale green fungus that remained on the surface as the matter transformed spread at lightning speed. Too fast to stop, to infectious to study safely. But it didn't send out spores, and it didn't creep along the ground, so once it dissipated it was safe to come near to do your duty to the Reset. That's what they called it. A Reset.

The off-worlders came to Reset the Earth. Rebalance the ecosystem so the energy the planet emitted didn't disrupt the proper flow of the universe. Those from outside our system but inside our galaxy learned over the ages to maintain the delicate dance of life. Travel as they'd done to reach us and begin the Reset was only affected in the direst of circumstances. So, there was no way to stop it. No way to convince them it wasn't needed because they only came as a last resort. The tended explained this to us once we'd stopped killing them. How much knowledge we'd lost in our initial futile attempts to stop the tide, no one knew.

   The delicate fronds of the plants that were once Jy and Raz waved in some unseen wind atop the small mounds that delineated where their human bodies once laid. I released the locket and slipped it back beneath the collar of my shirt and rose, following my team back towards the compound, looking out at the vast field of green and spindly arms of the trees growing from a thousand similar mossy mounds growing amidst the rubble of our pointless wars. A forest of memory. A forest of the fallen. I wondered how long they'd continue to hold their finger on the button. Clearing the planet of the hiccup and releasing the world to begin anew. I wondered if I would be here to see it. I pressed the heel of my hand to my locket and rubbed it lightly as I walked, and it stopped my morbid line of thought. That's why it was lucky. It reminded me of what mattered—love, family, humanity. What was and what could be. It cleared the badness away. Like pressing reset.

5

Apoptosis

The humming sound the ship made seemed muted after the cacophony of the battle. How long had it been? William couldn't remember. He blinked several times trying to clear his vision and his thoughts. A pod, he was in a pod. A shift of his eyes showed him almost nothing so he closed them again and tried to think, and remembered. He'd escaped. William's eyes darted around frantically as he assessed his position and realized what had to have happened. He stifled the urge to move or touch the controls, knowing his salvation lay only in inaction; if he fired the thrusters too soon, he might miss. It was hard, every instinct he had screamed for him to run as far and as fast as possible. Every bone in his body hurt, every muscle felt as if some mad and vicious thing had chewed on him and spit him out instead of swallowing. Bone-deep pain, the kind that lingered and followed you into the darkness of sleep, was his only companion. Shouting its presence in the silent blackness that grew larger and more encompassing as he drifted away.

The pod could have held more than one person. Three, tops, if they were small and there wasn't any other cargo. It held enough rations for two humans for a month, enough air and water for longer if you stayed calm and immobile. He'd once heard of someone who'd survived in a pod like this for almost an Earth year. They'd been in suspended animation and their oxygen requirements had been minimal in that state. Hopefully he wouldn't need to be here long. Hopefully someone safe found the vessel before he ran out of options.

It was comforting to know that he had options, unlike those he'd left behind. Though they were few, the reality of having more to look forward to than just death soothed him. A balm for his shattered nerves. He'd been tested beyond the realm of his previous imaginings by the last few days. Yet he'd learned how strong he was, how deep the determination to survive ran through his veins. If he closed his eyes now, he would probably see the faces of those he'd left behind in the ship. Their faces and what he'd done, how he'd changed them. Left his mark until nothing remained. Nothing human, that is.

William looked out the window at the rapidly retreating point of light that had been his home for more than two years. He should have felt something seeing it, from the knowledge that the light came from the incineration of the ship's interior fixtures, sealed away from the vacuum of space by the layers of metal and silicon composites that made up the hull. To the unaware it could be the normal lighting of the freighter. Not what it was, a metal tomb that burned merrily in place because there hadn't been a breach from the outside. No, destruction had come from within. He swallowed and looked up at his controls. His trajectory, providing he caught the solar wind stream it appeared that he'd aimed for, would take him on a long loop towards Mars and potential safety. If he didn't catch it, he still might get drawn into the slight gravity well of one of Mars' many moons. Which still offered him the chance for salvation, but it would take longer. Options. Paths to take, all of them leading away from what was into what might be. Built on the ashes of his former life. A life that ended in pain.

The pain was nothing compared to the fear. It was fear that held him immobile more than anything else. Fear that he hadn't left everything behind. Fear that something had clung to him or the pod, that something remained. Something that even now laid in wait for him to let down his guard so it could get in and do to him what it had done to his crew. For a moment all he could feel was the fear, that same suffocating madness that had been his constant companion for the last four days. When he'd begun to see the creatures lurking behind their eyes, begun to hear the faint hissing in their throats when they spoke. Watching them change, watching the metamorphosis, had stolen most of his logic. Stifled his ability to think, to reason. Trapped. He'd been trapped in the ship with them as they shifted from human to something other, and back again, before his eyes.

That was the worst part of this, beyond the pain, beyond the terror; the knowing that they had changed. That something had stolen who they were and now looked out of their eyes, speaking with the same voices but not. Knowing everything they knew but warping it, using it to further some agenda he couldn't fathom because he wasn't one of them anymore. He wasn't like them; they were new, and he had been left behind. Chosen to remain unchanged, unincluded in the newness of what they were. There hadn't been any choice really but to do what he'd done. None at all.

The panel before him beeped, and he struggled to lift his head to look at the readout. The pod wasn't automatic—he had to function, had to actively work the controls in order to do anything at all although it could be controlled remotely from the ship. He leaned forward slightly, his head spinning and vision greying out from the pain. Out of the corner of his eye he saw his reflection in the window. Something about it felt wrong. That thought sent adrenaline shooting through his veins. William turned his head, working to keep his breathing even, to not waste oxygen. Ignoring the now-steady beep of the panel, closing his eyes, he steeled himself then looked at his face.

Someone else looked back at him.

The scream built somewhere in his gut and erupted from his mouth before he registered the need to make a sound. It took him longer to realize the sound came from him. For a moment the horror of what he saw overwhelmed his senses and he struggled against the restraints on his chair, not remembering having fastened them but knowing he'd had to have done it; after all, no one had helped him into the pod. No one had been alive to help him. He'd killed them. Stabbed out their eyes to get at the things hiding behind them. Hiding in plain sight. He remembered using his slim metal knife, his arm moving again and again. The hot wash of blood and the stink of death mixing with the sanitizing agents the ship builders fused into the recyclers. They were dead, he'd had to kill them all because they'd changed and he hadn't, and no one would be safe until he removed the threat—the possibility of a threat—by removing them.

William stared, the steady beeping of the panel adding a throbbing counterpoint to the wild thudding of his heart as he struggled to regain his control and figure out what was wrong, what was different about the reflection he saw in the dull shine of the window. Terror swamped him, filling his nose with the scent of his sweat and the sour copper stench of blood until he felt the slim steady stream of tears falling and pooling on his chin. He tried to raise his hand to wipe them and realized he couldn't. Tearing his gaze away he looked down and saw that his arms were bound to the rests, restrained individually, one to each side. The crash restraints for jumps, locking his limbs in place to cushion and protect them from the g-force of high-speed maneuvers. Had he made a jump? The ship was too close, unless they'd followed him. NO. He'd killed them, he'd set the oxygen tanks to explode, and he'd gotten into the escape pod alone, that was the plan, he remembered it now. Because they were all dead. He closed his eyes, the tears falling faster, remembering Renate's face, the look of surprise as he'd thrust the knife into her eye and dug out what was hiding there. The look of fear and horror frozen in a single instant of pain, then nothing because her eyes were gone.

The beeping began to slow and he looked back at the console, his eyes drawn to the screen before him again. The usual display was replaced by a steadily decreasing series of numbers. A countdown. To what? He tried to remember. Renate, Xi, Morgan, Alf. Logan, Daniel. Screaming faces, missing eyes. Always the thing blocking them so they couldn't see him, didn't hear him or know him. He'd had to do it. Had to. The tears came faster, fell harder, and his chest hitched, his nose clogging shut as he moaned and cried into the stillness. His friends. His crew, like family. He shook his head to clear it and saw something else. Someone floating, tethered to the far end of the small cabin. Not in the other seat, but near the floor. Renate. As he'd seen her last. The empty sockets of her eyes blackened and shriveled, the edges crusted with dried blood. He wanted to scream but found he lacked the breath for sound. Lacked the breath because something was wrong with the air. He could feel it now, the heat and the scent of rotten eggs. The beeping distracted him again and William struggled to make sense of everything, but there were too many parameters. Too many questions and no answers, just the hollow sound of his shuddering tears and the beeping of the panel as it counted down.

His vision blurred again and he tried to shake his head to clear it, realizing his movements were slower. His eyes closed and he forced them open again, trying to remember what he'd forgotten. He needed to see, to make sure nothing remained so he could be sure he was safe. Was he safe? Did he get them all? He couldn't remember. He looked over at the floating form again. It was Renate. Her dead, empty eyes staring back at him accusingly. You did this, William. You. Cut the eyes from her head, stopped the beat of her heart. What did you see? Was it staring back at you in the window? He shuddered and tried to take a deeper breath, but couldn't; the air was wrong, but somehow that didn't scare him as much as it should have. He tried to smile.

"I had to, had to save you, Renate. Because I love you," he whispered, and closed his eyes.

The pod finally floated far enough away that they knew they would be safe. Daniel nodded to Xi, and she ran her fingers lightly over the screen, firing a single missile. She stared after it in silence like the other occupants of the room, the gravity of the moment too heavy for mere words. The bright flash of the explosion momentarily blinded them, and she blinked several times to clear her vision before standing and walking towards the door.

"We didn't have a choice, Xi. You know there's no hope once they have it." Daniel's voice halted her, and she looked back and nodded.

"He would have killed us all or given it to us, too. You did the right thing. Made the right choice," Xi said then left, and the others trickled out behind her. Daniel stared out the window, looking at the small cloud of debris spreading out in a circle from where the pod once floated. He was captain now. Not the way he'd thought to get the promotion, but William had caught it and there was no cure. Only one way to protect them all so far from home. Only one way to keep them all sane. The brutality of the solution left a sour taste in his mouth. William had been a good man once, a good friend. That was all just a memory now. Memory was what was left when nothing else stayed. A stain on the soul only time washed away. Pain and memory entwined, drifting away until only a ghost of it remained. Daniel activated the screens for the windows and turned to walk back to the upper deck, shaking off a bit of his melancholy in the need to do his duty. It would be another week before they were all in the clear and sure no one else had contracted the virus. For now, he would do what he needed to. He owed it to the rest of them to make do today. Answers would have to wait. He caught his reflection in the shining surface of the metal doors leading to the bridge. Was there something on his face?

PART TWO

IMAGININGS

Parallel: A Collection Of Science Fiction Short Stories

The stories in this section of the book are all what I would call Near Future imaginings. I took a look around and asked: What is the potential outcome of this thing we have going on right now? I asked myself where we might be in the next hundred or so years and twisted it to what is not likely but would be really wild. It's kind of hard to write dystopian literature with the way our world is going right now. You have to find the right balance of absurd and reality to keep things interesting. All of the stories in this section were first published on the VM site. Three of these: *The Call, Spin* and *Safe* were written in response to the found locket challenge And all of them started with me saying, Wow, that happened? Boy, wouldn't it be awful if...

7

Cake

They stood together at the end of a row in the center of the greenhouse. The red-tinged sunlight gleamed malevolently through the windows, heating the exterior into the triple digits. The greenhouse stayed cool, however, even though they could barely tell through the suits they wore. They worked in silence for a while, gathering, pruning, logging. An unending toil that paid off in weeks and months. Hours passed before he turned and spoke.

"How many quads are left?"

"Why are you asking me?"

"Because you care enough to keep track of it."

"Other people care."

"Not enough to keep track of it."

She frowned, unable to argue the point.

"15," she mumbled, and he looked up from his mound in surprise.

"I thought you said there were 16 last week."

"I did."

The silence after this statement lasted long enough that they both felt the weight. A quad going dark seemed inevitable. They didn't know that it was gone, they just knew it no longer responded. At least they didn't pretend anymore. Time was, they insisted you pretend you didn't know how many quads there were and that some were missing from the list. That was the thing about the world now. We'd stopped pretending. No more of the polite social lies and cognitive dissonance that ran rampant during the spiral to the end. It was the new age. We looked at what was and what would be and put the rest aside. It kept things simple. It kept folks sane. Wind whistled through the room, the automatic recirculation of the air that simulated a genuine summer breeze. It blew against their helmets and created a cocoon of sound that echoed in their ears, like when you picked up a shell on the beach and held it up to listen to the ocean. She wished she could take off her helmet and feel it instead of just hear it pass her. But she wouldn't be the one to contaminate their food; no one was foolish enough for that. Everyone knew what mattered. You worked together, you followed the rules.

"We're still here," she said, reaching out to pat his hand before rising to move to the next plant. Humans learned. We did. Slowly. We adapted, she told herself, looking out over the rows of seedlings stems stretching up towards the filtered sunlight coming through the greenhouse's glass roof.

"You can't make a cake without breaking a few eggs," she whispered, trying not to think of how long they had here. Hope felt pointless, the work felt pointless, but it wasn't. She knew that. It just got hard to remember sometimes.

"What's that?" he asked, and she shook her head, not willing to sink the mood any lower than it was.

"Think I might make a cake tonight. You want some if I do?" she said, and he smiled.

"What's the occasion?" he asked, and she shrugged.

"I dunno, Tuesday?" she replied, and he laughed, picking up his basket and walking over to put it on the conveyer.

"Those are my favorite types of occasions. The everyday ones," he said, and she smiled back at him, placing her own basket on the belt.

"Are you going to check the grid tonight?" he asked, and she nodded, the smile sliding from her face.

"After. Cake first. Then a little stream time, and if I'm not too tired I'll get to it," she said, and he nodded.

"Don't forget," he said, and she smirked.

"'Cause you care," she replied, and he grinned.

"Sure do. Just not enough to keep track."

8

Come Play With Me

The dog is large, and the girl is small. The pair looks harmless from a distance, and even more so up close. The girl's tattered dress is patched in places and ill-fitting, but clean. Like someone dressed in their finest after a long period of poverty and unrest for a ceremony of some sorts, or a party. The dog could be any breed, or all of them. Its features scream lovable mutt and its fur shines in a way that said someone's loving hands took the time to ensure it looked its best, down to the polka dot bowtie about its neck. They are a handsome pair, the kind that draws eyes and smiles and lowers defenses. You'd look at them and remember the things that were right in the world. The things that made you feel good, made you feel young.

The girl is small enough that when you see her you wonder if it is okay for her to be alone, but the presence of the dog allays concern. It tells you she is old enough to know, old enough for trust, because the dog is too big for her to handle unless she's had time and practice. When they walk nearer you hear her singing, and the sound of her voice is sweet and high, a happy child's voice; the voice of someone who, with time, could be something special. It has a tone to it, a note, that draws you in and pierces the dimmest, most jaded parts of you. It's the sound that makes the birds pause and then join in. They like it and complement it by singing along.

When she reaches the group of children standing by the playground, she pauses. Her dog stands just behind as if protecting or waiting for some signal, not tugging on the leash she holds loosely in her hand.

"Do you want to play?" the tallest of the children in the playground says, scratching absently at the sore on his arm. A thin line of pus leaks from it in reaction and the girl shrinks back a bit, her smile beginning to fade. The other children have sores, too. Some a few, some a lot. All of them stinking with rot. There are no sores on the girl.

"We're going for a walk; I have to keep moving *la dee dah dolly*, walking my buddy," the girl sings and the other children laugh, realizing she is younger than they thought and not smart enough for their games. The tall boy smirks and turns away, leaving her to walk on, the dog at her side sniffing the other children as they pass. *Not them*, he says and she nods, skipping now to speed away. Past the long line of houses on the rubble-strewn road.

There are few houses without some damage; most are fading and crumbling where they stand. Who cares to fix them when the world is fading? *La dee dah dolly*, fading away. The girl sings softer, slowing her skipping to a soundless walk, the dog following, tongue out, panting in the heavy early evening air. It's always hot now, and seldom humid. The air is full of scents and sounds, the sound and stench of decay. All things are breaking, what's left for remaking. *La dee dah dolly*, walking all day. The girl comes to a place blocked off from the road, a tall wall of cars and boxes barring entry to a cul-de-sac. She pauses by the barrier, humming softly. The dog starts his sniffing and gives a nod. She smiles and looks round for a way to enter, singing and humming as the dog sniffs the ground. There's a hole near the bottom too small for an adult, but just the right size for someone like her. Down on her knees, crawling now, softly, her eyes looking round as she hums to herself.

When she gets through, the dog crawls in after and the two stand quietly while she wipes the dirt from her hands. Her pretty dress has a spot that she frowns to see, but the dog is still sniffing so she follows him on. I think we have found them, oh yes we have found them. *La de dah dolly* found them at last. The girl resumes singing and alternates humming, and around her eyes, watching leveling guns.

"This is no place for children, pray where is your mommy?" a voice asks her softly from behind his long gun.

"Hither and there, she's watching me careful while I go out walking my buddy for fun." The sound of releasing and footsteps receding carefully greet her as the evening air hums.

"She looks clean," one man says and more people come out to and stare at and turn her in the soft setting sun.

"Did you lose your people?" A child comes to greet her, and the dog begins sniffing, oh yes this is the one.

"No, I know where they are, not far now, not far la *dee dah dolly*, my searching is done." The girls sings so sweetly and softly the people around her all lower their guns.

The dog resumes sniffing, his nose pressed and blessing each person who pets him with soft puppy hugs. What is better than a dog, tail wagging with love as he greets each new human to find what he seeks. A second and third child, their skin clear and eyes mild, come carefully out to meet the pair.

"Play with me please, come dance with my doggy and sing with me *la dee dah dolly* ho there."

"What's this about?" says one man with a shout as the children start spinning and floating on air.

"It's only to save them. The earth has naught for them, *oh la dee dah dolly* so have not a care." The girl's voice sang sweetly with sad screams receding as she and her dog rescue three more from there.

9

Labme #7

"Let me get yellow rice, spicy shrooms, Labme 7, and a side of pickled veg," the tall man said, impatiently rocking in place once the line moved and it was his turn to order. The thin woman behind the register raised an eyebrow.

"Labme 7?" she repeated, pausing and looking up at the man for the first time.

"Yes. What, are you out?" He laughed at his joke but no one around him smiled. Lab grown meat—or Labme as they called it—didn't need a farm. They made it in vats with the other proteins they couldn't grow, numbered it according to type. You really couldn't run out so long as there was a working computer and usable refuse. The woman directly behind him took a small step backward as if to give herself more than the required two-meter space.

"No, sir. Anything to drink?"

"Water," he replied, and the woman behind the register pursed her lips, typing in his requests.

"Fingerprint for the water. Face the camera for the rest. Your number is 32," the woman said as the light on the screen flickered from red to green when the camera scanned his face. The tall man placed his thumb on the keypad and snatched it away as it pricked him, drawing a miniscule amount of blood. He looked around nervously, then shrugged and walked off to wait for his order.

He ate alone and in silence with his eyes on his food, not looking up once. The water he consumed in small, reverent sips, eyes closed, savoring the purity of the unflavored liquid. He sat at a small table in the far corner of the dining hall and didn't notice that the space grew quieter around him. When he finished, he looked up and realized that he almost had the room to himself. A woman in a smartly fitted suit stood nearby, her face obscured by the mask covering her mouth, nose, and chin.

"Mr. Douglas. If you could come with me," the woman said, and he looked at her in surprise.

"What for?" he asked and looked closer, recognizing the uniform. Sweat gathered under his arms and on his upper lip. He wanted to wipe at his mouth but didn't, not wanting to draw attention to his face.

"Mr. Douglas, I am what we would call the easy way. I can leave and allow my associates to take you in. Their methods are not as agreeable as my own." She shrugged as she said this, her voice without inflection.

Greg Douglas darted his eyes around the room and saw that uniformed guards stood at every entry, their masks and matching uniforms a faded grey. He looked at her again and nodded, rising from his seat and leaving his tray behind on the table. She handed him a mask with her gloved hands—bright red and thick with no design—and waited while he hooked the elastic around his ears.

The walk to the elevator passed swiftly; he felt hemmed in by the trio of guards in front of and behind him as he followed the neatly dressed woman to the doors and inside the small car. The digital billboards in the elevator car cycled through their ads three times in the ride from the 10th floor down to the 30th. Greg watched the numbers with growing trepidation. Why had he done it? He'd heard the rumors, but he couldn't help himself. It was a craving. They'd told him it would come but he hadn't believed them, hadn't wanted to believe. Then couldn't stop himself from ordering it three days in a row.

The doors slid open, the quiet woosh overly loud in the silence. Only the sound of the Under and their echoing footsteps filled his ears as he followed the woman down the winding passage and into a small, sterile room. He'd heard about them but never seen them. There were so many rumors about what they did down here, in the government-controlled floors beneath the city. Down in the Under. They called it the Under because it was under everything. At the bottom of the whole world, and anything could happen here. Anything. A single chair sat bolted to the floor at the center of the room, over a shining metal grate. The walls of the room were clad with the same grey metal except for the large glass window the chair faced. The woman gestured for him to enter and stepped back, allowing him to pass and then closing the door behind him with a quiet clang and hiss.

He paced the room for some time before finally sitting in the chair. There was no sound from the speakers high on the wall; the window was black, as if waiting for someone to enter the room beyond. He sat nervously tapping his foot before rising again to pace the confines of the room, his mind racing. Why had had done it? He knew that was how they caught you. Even if there wasn't any proof, there were enough rumors saying the same thing that he'd suspected this one was true. It hadn't mattered. Didn't matter. Even standing in this room, waiting for god knows what, it didn't matter. He wanted more. He couldn't understand it. Hadn't been able to stop himself from asking for it again. The fabricators in his pod wouldn't make it. You could only get it in the dining halls. So they could track it. So they would know. He sat in the chair again, rocking a bit in the seat, wondering why they were making him wait.

"Number 7 is a test," a voice said, startling him from his reverie. He jumped out of the chair and wandered into the corner farthest from the mirror.

"What kind of test?" Greg asked, and there was a pause that went on so long he thought he'd imagined hearing the voice in the first place.

"The kind we use to sort. You know most people never have it again after the first time. We serve it to children to make sure we didn't miss, but sometimes things slip by. That's why it's an option in the dining halls."

"Things slip by?" Greg parroted and began to pace again, his mind turning the phrase over and over to find some meaning.

"Things," the voice repeated, and Greg reached up to touch the side of his face, the place where the thin skin-colored bandage covered the weird spidery rash.

"Why do you say 'things'?" he asked, but he knew; oh, he knew. His hands started shaking and he clenched them into fists, hiding them behind his back as if the cameras couldn't see. The cameras always saw. That's how they knew. No hiding here. No secrets except the most mundane.

"You can cooperate. Let us have it, Mr. Douglas. Let us take it alive so we can learn, and protect others from your fate." Greg backed away from the window until he hit the wall, a fine sheen of sweat forming on his skin despite the chill to the air.

"I don't know what you're talking about," he insisted, his voice barely more than a whisper. The low, derisive laugh that came through the speaker held a mocking tone that sent a chill down his spine.

"Oh, but you do. We will have it. The question is, will any part of you survive its removal? We can make it easy for you. A bit of light, a little nap, and in the end you're free."

"How can you be sure that I have it? How do you know?" He shook his head, trying to deny the inevitable. His finger throbbed in mockery of his questions. They knew, there was little chance they weren't sure.

"Come now. Don't be foolish, Mr. Douglas. Don't waste your time, you have so little left as you are now." Greg closed his eyes as anger rose in him, bubbling up like a fountain in response to the futility of it all. The isolation, the disembodied voice, all compounding the feeling of helplessness.

"Free? You say I'll be free? When you're going to make pudding of my brain to get at this thing? How can you even say it without laughing? How can you lie so easily?" Greg shouted, and began to pace in short angry strides—his fists beating at his legs in tandem with his steps.

"Free like we all are free, living in this stinking nightmare of a city, on the tiny strip of land left for humans on this godforsaken planet? Hiding from the things we created to save us? That kind of freedom? Or do you mean free of cares because I'll be a gibbering, drooling invalid without the capacity for deep thought and emotion, so I won't care anymore? Won't be able to care?" His voice rose to a fever pitch, his throat aching with the effort.

The silence in response to his outburst was not unexpected. When he calmed himself he walked over to the window and pulled the bandage off his face, exposing the rash to the unseen person or persons watching him. Then he turned and walked over to the chair, sat down, and began to cry. How long it lasted, he didn't know. His face felt swollen, and his shirt was wet along the hem where he'd used it to wipe at his eyes and nose during his fruitless fit of despair.

"Well, Mr. Douglas?" the voice questioned and Greg leaned his head back, closing his eyes and smiling bitterly.

"No, I think you're going to have to just kill me first. I'd rather not be around for the second act of this farce," Greg replied, sitting up to look into the darkened window. The lights came up and he could see a half-dozen officials and his wife seated in the room behind the window. His wife's face was pale, and her bottom lip trembled with the effort to hold back tears. He lifted a hand to his lips and blew her a kiss then nodded, and a green light illuminated him where he sat.

Then everything went dark.

10

Moon Bull

The thing you had to understand about the Lunar colony was that living on the moon itself wasn't the issue. They'd accounted for almost everything before they'd put the first human in the colony long term. The issue was keeping things alive. The domed colony could almost pass for a city on Earth. It certainly tried, with its roads and parks and open-air vistas. The bubble was and remained the epitome of sustainable engineering. On paper, the colony could survive indefinitely. Yet in reality, in practice, things died. The moment they planted anything other than trees and grass in the carefully prepared soil, the timer started. The moment anyone and anything set foot on the surface, the hourglass started dribbling sand. Which made the bull so odd.

It started as a joke, really. A nursery rhyme made real. You put people on the moon, you had to have a cow. The cow jumps over the moon, you know. All you needed then was a hyena and bit of imagination. It made for great publicity for the colony, too. Scientists trying to figure out how to enable large mammals to live in the lunar colony. They'd already made adaptions to several other animals' DNA to send those up. Long-extinct arctic birds, fish, etc. Trying to recreate home on our tiny rocky satellite. Folks voted on the names—Dick and Jane, Belle and Beau, Skeeter and Dolly. A long list of horrid and hilarious entries, with the worst of them winning. Blue the bull and Cheese the cow. They fiddled and fussed and broadcasted the entire saga, from in-vitro implantation of the genetically altered bovine embryos, to their birth on the moon. Their Earth-born mother died right after they were weaned.

Cheese lived two years. She'd grown and thrived for the first fifteen months like a normal cow. Seeming to easily adapt to her lunar home. Then she'd stopped eating.

Stopped doing anything, and poor Blue spent every day bringing her hay and nudging her to get up. When she died folks mentioned how the moon seemed to kill things, but they didn't dwell on it. After all, they'd done everything right in creating it hadn't they? Blue survived. He mourned Cheese for months, walking every morning to her enclosure and letting out a long low moo before trudging on to the field of genetically modified grasses where he spent his days grazing. After some time, his caretakers noticed he'd stopped going to her pen, but if he chanced to pass it he'd stare mournfully at the empty stall before moving on.

It went on like that for years. Until someone finally realized that Blue never seemed to get any older. Had to have been his fourth or fifth set of caretakers who'd pointed it out. Every five years someone would say, well why don't we see about getting him some company? Then the debate would start raging, about the costs and feasibility and the way things didn't last on the moon.

That's how they talk about it. They say things don't last. Never any successful pregnancies that start on the lunar surface. Never any old people that weren't already old before they got there. The moon is for visits. Everyone knew you didn't stay. If you stayed you didn't last. Except Blue. So, they took to rotating out his caretakers after ten years. Except no one seemed to realize bulls don't live more than 20 years on Earth. Then someone pointed out the fact that they'd been rotating his caretakers for going on 30 years. So, they started to study him. Took his blood once a week and monitored how much he ate, the size and shape of his poop—you know, normal science things. They couldn't explain it. And after a while they left it alone. He seemed to dislike it when they bothered him too much. He just liked to watch the way the humans and the few other species of animals living in the colony lived their lives.

I started visiting him when he was around fifty in Earth years. I'd been working for the International Space Association for ten years before even setting foot on the moon. I remember it like it was yesterday. The seemingly endless rounds of shots and tests before the quick flight up from the Low Earth Orbit Station. My woefully brief tour of the colony. Every day I was there I'd go visit his enclosure; Blue would tilt his head and look at me when I greeted him, so I took to talking to him like I'd talk to anyone. Telling him about the changes in the colony, the way things stood back on Earth. Just small talk really. He didn't seem to mind. He stayed close enough to listen and chewed on some bit of something, occasionally shaking his head as if something I'd said amused or surprised him. I enjoyed the peacefulness of our one-sided conversations, the simple understanding I saw in his big bovine eyes, so the next time I came up I went back.

I kept it up for a good 30 years, until they told me I wouldn't be able to make the trip anymore and wanted me to retire. I still felt young despite not looking it, but times had changed. They'd become more cautious about who they allowed into the colony, about how long you could stay and what you could do when you got back. The last time I saw him I told him about it. Told him how something had spooked them, made them want to abandon the colony for good. Of course, they couldn't. Didn't they need humans up here with the plants and animals they'd adapted to live with them there? But that was an argument for younger people. I said my goodbyes to Blue, and he did something surprising: he came over and pressed his big nose into my hand. Somehow, he'd understood he wouldn't be seeing me anymore.

I heard last year that they were rotating his caretakers every five years now. Not that it mattered. I was content to know he was being cared for by someone, even if they didn't last. He seemed happy every time I saw him. Carefree even, despite being so alone. I told my grandson he was close to 80 now and had already outlived everyone who'd been there when he was born. Of course, he didn't believe me. Everyone thought they just named every bull on the moon Blue. Everyone knew the moon sucked the life out of things. Except that bull. Yup. He's an odd one.

11

Spin

Who's gonna spin, gonna spin, gonna spin.
Spin away the pain, all the pain, all the pain.

The song echoed in the darkness, and they followed the sound downwards, past the parts they liked to visit, past the parts they pretended they didn't, into the places they only went when forced. Their footsteps were barely audible over the blaring of the music, and the cloying scent of decay grew stronger the further down they traveled. They'd been searching for hours, hours longer than they had to stop the dance.

When they found him, it was too late; he sat tailor-style in a corner, his blood spilling out in a slowly spreading pool and his stained fingers fisted around something he held pressed close to his chest. His victims lay in a macabre circle around him, their own puddles long cold and sinking slowly into the dirt floor of the cave.

Give the gift of blood, blood, blood. Give the gift of pain.

The only god lies in the knife, we use to play this game.

The speakers on his holo played the tune in a loop as he sat rocking in his puddle, clench-fisted and drooling as his life ebbed out around him.

"Turn that crap off," Detective A said, and one of his team walked over to where the murderer had dropped the holo and used the edge of his jacket to shut it down. The silence suited the mood better than the ditty. The trio stood staring down at the man, disgust plain in their expressions.

"You'd think everything blowing up would have stopped this kind of thing," C said, pulling out his handheld to run the camera over the scene.

"The more things suck, the more folks want to escape," B replied, shaking his head and using his own handheld to call for a cart, stepping backwards to stay out of the frame of C's camera.

"And why should the end of the world stop humans from doing what they always do? This poor sap probably never even noticed the rest of the world had gone to shit. Business as usual for him. Same as us," Detective A said, crouching to look at the dying man.

"Why'd you do it, huh? We're already fighting to survive down here. What was it, punk? You on *the Spin*?" A asked, not expecting an answer. The guy looked too far gone, and touching him wasn't an option. No clue what he had, what he'd been into this far down. The rocking motion was slowing now but the man lifted his eyes to look at them, still somehow aware despite being so far gone.

His eyes had the telltale tinge and A shook his head, rising to go stand next to the entrance of the chamber. It always ended the same. Even in this new reality, this new world where humans were few and codependent. Except some folks never really fit in, did they? Considered excess and not assigned. What choice did they have? Starve or Spin.

Still, there should be rules. There should be order. Even if we're all circling the drain, we should wait our turn and not jump the queue. Not push others out of the line before their number is called. Otherwise, it isn't fair. And shouldn't something be fair? That's why he wore the uniform. Detective A pulled out his stick and lit the end, taking a deep drag of the sweet-smelling herb, allowing the smoke from the faintly laced leaves to do its job: Relax him and block the smell and bitterness of the situation.

The junkie's rocking slowed to a stop as A took another long pull on his stick and closed the cap to save it for later. His thoughts began to even out and he nodded to some thought only he could hear.

"Okay, guys, you got what we need?" B and C nodded, as disappointed as he at the fact that there wasn't anything left to do. That they'd arrived too late to save anyone again. He turned to walk back out the way they'd come in. Damn shame. Even if they weren't living above the line, their lives mattered. Now, because one selfish bastard wanted dance partners, they had a half-dozen bodies in the Under while the sky bled up above. Maybe that's why he did it. Took a *Spin* and grabbed a few friends. The whole world was on fire and the rivers ran with blood. The rich pushed the poor lower and deeper to make room as more of the land above became uninhabitable in their war. What did someone like him have to hold on to? The knife he'd used to carve up those pretty girls? The hope that, once the governments stopped fighting, they'd leave those of us still living alone to rebuild in peace? Who knew, and it didn't matter now.

"*Dance like it matters, spin in the sun. Dance like it matters till your life is done,*" the man said from behind them, his voice barely a whisper as he unclenched his hand and let the object fall free. His head lolled to the side like a broken doll as his chest collapsed with his final exhale. The trio turned to watch, staring until they were sure he was gone, then Detective A walked a bit closer to see what he'd dropped. A locket. Had he stolen it from a victim? Did it matter, now that they were gone? They left it and the rest where they lay. The cart would be there when it came. Later rather than sooner, this deep in the Havens. B began to whistle as they moved briskly back up through the remnants of their civilization. *Who's gonna spin* he whistled, moving past the ones who didn't matter to anyone but themselves.

Moving up closer to the light, but not out. Never out. After all, the sky was still bleeding, and it wasn't time for them to leave the dance.

12

Safe

"Someone smart might worry about where their gloves are, not a useless bit of jewelry," Leigh said, holding mine up as I crawled along the floor of the tiny room we called home, looking for my locket. I tossed her a smile over my shoulder but didn't stop my search. I wasn't leaving without it; I needed it for later. I found it wedged in the corner, obviously having fallen behind the table when I'd removed it last night. Smiling, I fished it out and held it up for her to see.

"It fell, looks like someone knocked it off the table when I was making her scream last night." I smirked as I said this, fastening the locket around my neck so it hung between my breasts and pulled on my shirt. Leigh walked over and wrapped her arms around my waist for a quick hug, then moved to the other side of the room—four whole steps—to let me finish rubbing down my face as I'd rubbed the rest of my skin with odor neutralizing cream. I saturated the peach fuzz on my head with the thick sweat-blocking gel I kept in the large container on the sink before sliding my balaclava over my head, with the mask part bunched under my chin until I needed it, and tucked everything in. Then I checked again, making sure my base layer had no tears or snags before I pulled on my jeans, boots and jacket, and took the gloves from her outstretched hand.

"You set, hon?" I asked, running my eyes over her quickly and smiling with relief. Leigh wasn't always careful.

"Absolutely. Do you know what sector they have us in today?"

"D-16. Over by the library." I smiled as I told her, knowing she loved the crumbling old building despite the fact that it no longer held books. She took my hand as we locked up and made our way through the winding corridors to the exit, the rumble of the building's mechanics a quiet backdrop to the sounds of the high-rise city. It was the sound of safety. It no longer felt odd, living life largely indoors.

I gave Leigh's hand a squeeze before releasing it to slide on my gloves and pull up my balaclava as our unit commander handed out the lightweight scent suits we wore over our clothing. Fifty years ago, they'd called them Haz-mat suits. But humans tend to distill things down to their most basic functions. The suits didn't just block the pathogens in the air; they sealed in our scents, which was equally important. So now they're called scent suits. I turned and allowed Leigh to check the seals on the back of my neck and ankles while I checked my front then did the same for her, affixing the Velcro edges to our gloves and giving her the thumbs up signal as I pressed my chin to my neck to activate the comm so we could talk.

"Ready?" I asked, and she nodded, half listening to our commander give his normal safety speech; the one he'd sent as part of the email this morning when we'd received our assignments, so I wasn't missing anything by not listening. It only deviated in minor ways from the speech he'd given every day this week. It was a wonder we didn't recite it with him, but our listening to his recital was part of the ritual. Humans loved rituals. I should know, since I had been waiting for him to reassign us to D-16 for weeks so I could do my own. Rituals let us know something important was about to happen. In the case of our commander, it was to let us know we were going outside. As he spoke the hum started, first a pulse then a revolving tone that built, and would have drowned out his voice had it not piped directly to our ears. I barely noticed the hum, impatient to start the day.

The decon cycle began with a whoosh of sanitizing gas that filled the bay and wound me tighter than a spring. Going outside was always complicated. I can remember when we didn't need all of this. I'd been six when the first ones escaped, and we'd learned to fear. Fear the scratching that preceded the attack, fear the horrid gasping death. I'd watched the whole world change. Things were better now. Thirty years later, we'd regrouped and rebuilt.

The whirring hum jumped to a high-pitched screech, and we turned up the volumes on our comms to compensate. Once it reached operating levels it would barely be audible to human ears, but not theirs. Those tiny pointy-eared bastards hated the sound enough to give us a wide berth when it was at daytime levels; keeping them far enough away to protect the wiring from their teeth and tiny agile fingers was crucial to our survival. Hence the need to go out daily to lay traps and keep them back away from our settlements. Away from the high-rise cities that housed the remnants of humanity.

I hopped into the driver's seat of our cart and waited as Leigh and the other two members of our squad settled and strapped in. The antechamber that housed the carts had large glass doors that folded open accordion style to allow the electric vehicles to roll in and out as needed. I was glad they'd added the Squeal to our carts, too; another layer of safety for my crew. Everything worked together. The Squeal, the Pits, the Scent Suits, the Burns. It kept us safe from the Swarms, although nothing could really keep them away. But this allowed us to have lives again. Living in the new norm. And that's just what I planned to do.

We cleared two buildings before we got to the library. I assigned the other two members of the team to take the upstairs and had Leigh join me in clearing the downstairs. There were only four buildings standing in this sector, and it was almost ready for demo. I knew I'd feel more secure when they were down. I breathed easier when I could see. See the land around me, unimpeded. No holes and bushes for things to hide. No walls and rubble for them to climb. No tall grass or unpaved ground. Just clear, pristine panels as far as the eye could see.

"I want to show you what I found last time," I said, gesturing for Leigh to follow me. When we reached the back of the building, beyond the endless rows of empty shelves, I gestured for her to wait then reached into the niche of one of the long tables to out the small painting I'd found hidden in the rubble.

"Is that what I think it is?" Leigh asked, surprise evident in her voice.

"It is. An actual oil painting. I wanted you to see it before they destroyed this place. I wanted you to hold it while I asked you."

"Asked me what?" Leigh said, tilting her head. I wished I could see her face, but the masks made it impossible.

"To make it formal, you and me. There's too little beauty in the world. But that right there, it's almost as beautiful as the way you make me feel."

She nodded, and I saw the flaw in my plan: with our Scent Suits on I couldn't kiss her. Couldn't even hold her, but I could make up for it later. My comm beeped and we moved to the cart, giving the 'all clear' and riding back to the city while the Squeal ramped up to clear the areas around the Pits before the Burns started. When we'd checked in and decontaminated, I pulled her up to the glass-domed rooftop garden and we moved among the trees, watching the Burn and hearing the inevitable screeching of the rats that had made it far enough into the pit to fall victim to the flames. The smell and sight of it was ugly, but up here the air was clear, and Leigh was beautiful. She wore my locket around her throat and her clean-shaven head sported just a bit of my lipstick, the part I missed when I'd kissed her after fastening the chain around her neck. I could see for miles. The swiftly growing forest, the Barrier Plain, the Pit and its smoking ring of black around the Haven. Sure, tomorrow they might send me to a building that held a nest of the Swarm. Or maybe I would tear my suit and get a choice between slow or quick. But today, right now, everything was beautiful. And I felt safe.

13

The Call

The doorbell rang just as the family was sitting down to dinner. They weren't expecting anyone, so Miriam pulled out her tablet to look at the doorbell app. It was a delivery courier. With a sigh she rose and went to answer the door herself, unsure what could be coming so late at night. She opened the door and gave a small, polite smile—the kind of smile she reserved for unwanted visitors and salespeople who are too pushy.

The courier standing on the rubberized solar mat in front of her door simply asked her to verify the address and handed her a small square package, holding his tablet up to scan her face for verification of delivery. She blinked and looked at the label, then opened her mouth to speak, but the courier had already turned away and was walking briskly back down the short flight of stairs leading to the sidewalk outside. The puffy square mailer was light enough to be empty, and didn't make a sound as she carried it to the dining room and placed it on the slim oak sideboard she'd inherited from her grandmother years ago.

"What was that, Mom?" her son James asked in between bites of his food. Miriam sat down and placed her napkin in her lap before taking a sip of her wine.

"Your uncle got a package," she replied, picking up her fork and looking across the table to where her brother sat. He raised an eyebrow but she didn't say anything more, tucking into her dinner with a focus that discouraged conversation.

The package sat on the table, very much the center of attention despite being out of most of their direct line of sight. Politeness dictated that they finish dinner first. It belonged to her brother, and no one could ask about it without seeming rude. Yet it was there. Miriam made a show of eating, chewing deliberately slow, savoring each bite and swallowing without pause—her eyes fixed either on her plate or on the wall above her brother's shoulder. Levi sighed, putting down his fork and rising to go see what it was. His hand began to tremble the moment he saw the label, but he clenched his fingers and snatched the package up before he could lose his nerve.

With his back to the room he opened it, saw the slim box and neatly folded letter and closed his eyes, unwilling to take the last few steps but knowing he had to. Steeling himself, he unfolded the letter and read the three short lines then used the tip of one finger to pry off the lid on the box and peek inside before shoving everything back into the mailer and returning to his seat.

"What was it, Dodh Levi?" James asked as his uncle took a long sip of his water and resumed eating.

"My locket came; it would seem our time together is at an end." Miriam made a low noise that sounded a lot like a curse, but didn't stop eating. It was clear she wanted to pretend things were normal.

"This is the Calling Year for balance, right? And everyone with the locket has to go away?" James asked, nodding as he spoke, reciting the words like he'd learned them—tonelessly and precisely. As if something so terrible could bypass normal human emotions.

"That's right," Levi replied, pushing his food around his plate.

"Where does everyone go?" James asked, and his mother made a low hissing noise that made him look at her instead of his uncle.

"Well, they never told us that part. They just told us you had to go but not always, so maybe he doesn't have to go, right? If we tell them we don't want him to?" James said, but his mother was already shaking her head.

"It is a rare thing to get a locket and get to stay. Only the wealthy or important ever get to pass their lockets to another. Each locket must have a person," Miriam said, rising to clear the table and give herself some time. Time. Something they took for granted usually. Now the clock had run out.

"Uncle Levi is important."

"To us. Not to the world. You must be important to the world for the locket to pass," Miriam said as her eyes began to fill. She turned away and walked into the kitchen, the unfairness of the situation turning into a hot ball of anger and despair that lodged itself in her throat and threatened to choke her.

"Even if I was I couldn't, little one. My locket is gold." Miriam gasped as her fingers went numb with shock and the plates she held clattered to the floor.

"Gold!!" She shook her head as rage stole the ability to speak for a moment.

"Every ten years! And somehow it is the poor and unconnected who end up culled without even the option to pass their locket to another. Meanwhile the rich linger on, draining the world of every bit of life. Growing old, enjoying their families."

"Don't stir up tsuris, Miriam. It is my time. I have lived a good life. We do our part. We accept the Call. So there is a future, so we hold back the end and turn the tide."

"Seems to me it is only the ones who don't cause the leaks that end up being the bricks used to fix the dam," Miriam said but nodded, stooping to pick up the plates and clean the mess, when Levi shook his head again.

"Where do they go, Dodh?"

"Every year when people reach their 69th birthday they receive their locket. And on the Calling Year those with lockets go to the culling field. There they are reclaimed and used to plant a forest to heal the planet," Levi said, putting a nice face on the fact of his death. Omitting the fact that those with gold lockets aren't always only the old. Some people got a locket for other reasons and didn't always get to wait until the Calling Year. Some went to the culling field the moment their use to society ended because of catastrophic illness or making the wrong enemies. His locket should have been silver. He should have another ten years, but no.

"I don't want you to go, Dodh, but I am glad you will make the balance. It's how we make things right," James said, eyes shining with tears and something else. Fanaticism? Faith? Levi didn't know, but he caught his sister's eyes over the boy's head and frowned. She shook her head and he nodded, knowing that the schools made sure to teach them why this was needed. Why they came up with this way to control the population and reverse the damage to the planet. But the cost was steep. And the irony steeper. The system is so fair, so just. So rigged.

"I don't want to go either, James, but I will. As will you one day. So tomorrow, I will put on my locket and go. You and your mother will kiss me goodbye and remember me. And in a few years, maybe you come see my tree, yes?"

James nodded and Miriam turned to go back into the kitchen to cry. She'd never hated anything as much as she hated those lockets.

Parallel: A Collection Of Science Fiction Short Stories

PART THREE

ENVISIONINGS

Parallel: A Collection Of Science Fiction Short Stories

While the stories in the first two sections of this book are only loosely related by theme or genre, the stories in this section are all part of my worldbuilding process for my upcoming science fiction series. The idea for the world came years ago at the start of my professional writing journey, with a short story call from a small press located in Texas named Balance of Seven. I envisioned a world where humans have spread out into the Sol system and are doing what humans always do. But the creation of this world meant I had to first ask the question: how did we get there? I wrote two other stories "The Job" and "Trues", which at first glance wouldn't seem to fit together at all. But once I got going and asking what if, it all seemed to come together.

In the middle of all this thinking I met a couple of guys named Teman and Shaun. We all answered a call to be a part of a writer's collaborative, only the guys wanted to be the next Stan Lee without understanding (or researching) what that meant. We split off almost immediately and spent a year working on what we eventually came to call the Zero Hour Archive. Those two were mad for writing about the whys and philosophical pitfalls of the world we created together. But like all group projects, there's always a clash of wills. At the end of the year, I looked at what we'd done and realized that some of what we'd all envisioned together would fit quite nicely into the world of *The Parallax Saga*, where "Seiryuu's Fire" took place. I revamped the stories I wrote with those guys and melded them into the timeline and world I was creating, and voilà! I have something that if not for two hard-headed philosophers, a duo of ladies in Texas, and one fireball life coach named Debbie stuck out in Mormon country would not be as full and interesting as it is now. I ordered the stories in this section chronologically, not in terms of publishing order as only three of the stories in part three are available elsewhere ("The Job", "Enhanced", and "Trues".) but in the chronology of my imagined world. A world where we continue as we are and things get worse, way worse, until they get better and transform over a period of 300 years. Humans will likely take that long to get their act together. But even when we do, the one thing we won't stop being is us.

15

Sanitation 6

The LEDs were set to moonlight, and Marcus was dreaming about bread. Not just any bread, but bread from the Jewish deli in New York. The one that had been in the same spot since before they erected the Liberty Island sea wall. A loud beep sounded, and he realized it wasn't a car horn, but an alarm. Opening his eyes, he stared around in confusion before he remembered where he was. Looking at the clock, he realized he had two more hours until shift end, so he got up and snagged an energy drink from the mini fridge in the corner of his office and took it back to his desk. Across the room, the other members of his team sat in front of their triple monitor setups, culling the code for intrusions and hiccups and studiously ignoring the beeping noise.

"Someone check that, will you?"

"Aww, did the loud beeping noise disturb your nap, oh mighty Marcus?" Daisy replied, and he snorted.

"You'll get your turn next," he quipped, and she shook her head.

"I don't sleep at work, and frankly I'm not sure why you risk it with all the cameras about," she said, and he smiled.

"It's not much of a risk this time of night. Plus, I have a deal going with a guy up in HR. He hooks me up. I just have to give him the signal. He can do it for you, too. Up votes with a C?" Daisy rolled her eyes in response to that, then frowned.

"Sanitation 6 has an error code," she said, peering at her display.

"Where is that one located?" he asked, pulling the tab on the can and raising it to his lips for a long swallow.

"Green sector up on 10 central."

"Pull the feed." He moved to stand next to her and look over her shoulder at the screen. Something obscured the lens, a splatter which provided a cloudy view of the area just in front of the industrial floor vac robot set to clean the larger common areas.

"Looks like a wet patch. That's near the smoothie stand. One of the users must have dropped a shake. Cue up the spills team and give me a wide angle on the area so I can tell if vac ran over something too thick."

Daisy typed a bit and then moused over, so one of her screens displayed the feed from the overhead cameras in the green sector. The bot had stopped in the corner where plants and a few chairs obscured the area behind it. Daisy pulled up a different camera to get a closeup and zoomed in.

"Can we get sound on this?" he asked. Daisy shook her head. The scene playing out before him was unbelievable. A man in a facilities maintenance uniform was struggling to free a woman from the bot. The woman was offering no help, her body flopping against his efforts and the suction of the machine. The spill in question was her blood.

"Holy fu—" Daisy said, and Marcus echoed her sentiment, the two of them staring in horror as the tech slipped and fell, then stood and began tugging frantically again. Blood splattered every time he slipped, but still the woman didn't wake or assist him with saving herself from the machine.

"Why didn't he push the abort button? Where's his partner?" Marcus asked futilely. Obviously, if he'd had help, he would have called it. The suction on the bot was so powerful if he let go, the thing would grind her up and suck her in, bit by bit. The mop-vacs were almost like lawnmowers that way. Designed to cut up debris and shunt it into its holding bin for emptying. He'd heard the techs had complained it was overkill, that someone could get hurt if a hand got caught, but they'd brushed those concerns away. "Havasupai must be clean", was the mantra.

"Is he wearing his headset?" Marcus asked, and Daisy tried to zoom in on his face, not seeing the telltale cord at his neck.

"Doesn't look like it. We need to route security to help," Daisy said, and Marcus nodded, then realized he would have to notify the higher-ups.

"Do that. This is above our band for sure, and definitely out of our lane. I'll call and apprise the department head of the situation," Marcus said, watching as the tech slipped again, then tore his eyes away from his screen to go back to his desk. Out of his lane. When had he started parroting that crap? It felt wrong but it had flowed out his lips like he was reciting times tables in 3rd grade math class. His display had a dozen blinking flags. As he moved to address the first, his screens went dark.

Then the lights went out.

For several long moments, as the complete blackness settled in, he sat in silence. Shock locking his body in place. Havasupai. The city of the future. The country's first Earth-Sheltered city, built miles underground at the edge of the Grand Canyon. Artificial light was essential. The sun couldn't reach this far underground. Without it the darkness wasn't just complete, it was entombing. Like a blanket of night that smothered all your senses except your ears. He could hear the computers and the HVAC system. The breathing of his coworkers on the other side of the room. He could hear his heartbeat thundering, picking up speed with every passing moment. Then there was a loud beep—the signal of something being reset, the auto kicking in—and the room brightened again. But his computer screens remained dark.

"You got anything?" he asked, and Daisy shook her head. Marcus looked over at the other occupants of the room—Mike and Laurie. They shook theirs, too. The system was down, but at least the lights were back on.

"I'm going to call main." He looked down at his phone. The Wi-Fi was down. Something that should have been impossible in a place with so many redundancies. He got up and paced the room. They couldn't see what was happening. Someone needed to notify security. That tech needed help.

"Any of you guys have a signal?" he asked, knowing it was futile. Their phones were all provided by the same carrier; same models, same features. Standard with their uniforms and positions at Havasupai. Standing. He nodded to himself. He was in charge. He had to take action, so he would.

"Okay, Mike, you keep trying to get us back online. Go over to the servers and do a manual reset if need be. Laurie, do what you do best. Daisy, fiddle with the walkies. Maybe we can get those working in the short term. I'll take one of them with me. I'm heading up to ten to press that damn button." A combination of relief and fear washed over the faces of the others at his words.

Marcus headed down the hall and over to the line of elevators leading to the bridges and Central. IT was floors lower and on the east side of the city, so the walk was not short. He considered taking the stairs but knew time was of the essence, and as out of shape as he was he'd likely have a coronary trying to run up so many flights of stairs.

Time seemed to crawl as he walked, then waited for the elevator and walked some more until he reached Green sector. Only to find he'd arrived too late to be of any help. Nothing remained of the scene he'd seen on the monitor except for a few hazard cones and blood.

In person, it was even more grisly. The coppery scent of death hung heavily in the air atop the normal smells of Havasupai. That was the thing about the city. You spent the first two weeks acclimating to the way it smelled. No matter what they did, they couldn't eliminate the whole 'cave' vibe. Earth has a scent. Eons of organic matter and decay. The smell of mud and minerals. They'd covered the lot with something they called 'summer wind', a fragrance that was supposed to smell like the air at the ocean on a clear day. The reality was less than successful, though it wasn't as bad. Not like in the beginning. The first weeks before the HVAC system had been fully operational, everything smelled like a fish market in late August. He smelled none of it now. Just the blood.

Marcus looked around, trying to figure out what had happened. There was no sign of the worker, the victim, or the bot. No footprints or handprints in the blood, just a few puddles and leftover smears. Clearly, someone in one of the other hubs had keyed in and taken care of things. But how could they have with the systems down? Outages were the norm, but when one went out they all went out. They were still setting things up, after all. He stared harder, thinking. They'd designed everything for integration and seamless function. This had all the earmarks of ConNext efficiency. Like always, when a problem cropped up, someone swooped in and handled it, so everyone was free to think of something else.

He stood in place for a moment, wondering if he should do something more, if he could do anything at all. If anyone would know, they'd be in the ConNext offices on the other side of Central.

As he walked, he saw more hazard cones and no people. Given the hour, he expected light crowds—it was just a bit past 4am, but there should have been someone around. Havasupai was like any city. Someone was always up. All the lights in the office's front were dim except the entry panel, and he could see someone sitting at the reception desk at the rear of the space. Walking up to the door he pressed the button for entry, surprised when the line clicked open but not the door.

"Yes?" a voice made tinny with electronics and irritation replied in response to his summons.

"I'm Marcus Courson, IT supervisor in Sector Two. I came up to help with the incident because our systems are down."

"They handled the incident. You can return to your post."

"I know, I mean—I can see it's no longer urgent. I just wanted to know if the woman is okay."

"We're not open at the moment. Perhaps you could come back during normal business hours. Or leave a message with your admin team. Have a great evening."

The line clicked off and Marcus stood staring at the panel as if that could force the person who'd answered to open the door. To tell him something. He looked down at his phone; still no signal. Shrugging, he trudged back to the elevators, deep in thought. It was possible he could get a signal on the surface. If he went up and walked closer to the tower, he could probably get a clear line to ConNext, his lab, and even the police. Matching thoughts to words, he jogged to the elevators and rode them to the top.

Havasupai used to be part of the Treaty Lands, a thriving town near the national park with a waterfall for its major attraction. Climate change had ended that. Now it was just a small group of buildings with a few scrawny trees sitting back from the entrance to the underground city. The designers had sought to create a natural, almost park-like setting to house the entrances to the complex. Identical buildings to the one he stood in front of sat at each cardinal direction, each with its own the cell tower and plant. They'd recreated what they lost ten years prior with specimens of the trees and other foliage in a well-tended but compact memorial garden. The blackened remains of the wildfires had made this new city not just possible, but necessary.

In the twilight hours, where sunrise is not far off and the moon has just begun to set, the desert is a lonely place. The only light came from the slim solar strips carved into the ground and the buildings themselves. Marcus stood staring silently out into the distance. Nothing stirred. Just miles of emptiness punctuated by the occasional call of a coyote. Arizona differed from New York. And this place differed from the rest of the state. The builders had wanted to create a scaled-down version of Phoenix miles underground, but it didn't quite succeed. You always knew exactly where you were, especially since there were cameras and ConNext posters everywhere. He missed the sounds and smells of New York. The bustle of millions of people surviving and thriving a hair's breadth away from the fragile looking sea wall that managed the ever encroaching water's rise. He missed the quirky stores and restaurants selling handmade goods. Taking this job had been great for his wallet, but he paid in ways he hadn't expected. Marcus took a moment to breathe, then checked his signal and saw he had full bars. Dialing the main line he tried to get through to ConNext, wading through the auto to leave a message for Ryan, his team admin. Something like this required direct communication, and he was enough of a team player that he couldn't let him go into this without all the info. They would want to know what he saw and what they'd done.

Someone should call the police.

His fingers hesitated over the numbers. He had reason to hesitate. He'd signed so many nondisclosure agreements. They'd made it clear that what happened here stayed here. Calling when he didn't have the full information and knew nothing couldn't help anyone. Yet his instinct was there. It's only natural, after all. When there's an accident of this sort, you call for help. The police department hadn't yet finished setting up their station here, and the hospital was still under construction. They still depended on the surface for help with big things. Maybe help had already come. What could he offer but another piece of the puzzle? An incomplete piece because of the power loss. He knew the way the city worked, the way

ConNext worked. They would handle it in-house, had always handled it in-house. The lack of body, the missing janitor, it all tracked. That woman had needed help. And ConNext only really helped itself. Before he could stop himself he hit send on the call.

"Hello 911, please state the nature of your emergency."

"Hello, yes, I'm out at the new city — Havasupai? Has anyone called about the acci—" he started, and the line cut out. He pulled his phone away from his ear and looked to see if he'd lost the signal, but he still had the full set of bars. Marcus raised a hand to his mouth, chewing absently at the end of his thumbnail, then dialed again. This time, the call didn't ring. He held his phone up to his face, glaring at the screen for a long moment. There was no reason, none at all, for his phone to cut out. Unless.

Unless.

He ruthlessly shut down that line of thought. Uncertainty held him immobile. What did he know? Nothing really. So he should go back to work despite the growing fear making him feel sick to his stomach. Shrugging it off, he turned and went back into the building, riding the elevator back down to Central and pulling out his tablet. He took the long way so he wouldn't have to go past the accident scene, noting that security guards were patrolling, preventing anyone from entering the hub. Seeing the guards with their ConNext security uniforms and high-tech accessories did little to reassure him. Where were the police?

By the time he'd gotten to the elevators closest to his department, he'd convinced himself that the outages and the accident had little to do with one another. The thing was, in life, the simplest explanations were probably the correct ones, even if they seemed implausible. Humans were superstitious by nature, and prone to herd-like reactions to danger and upset. Given the distance from the next city and the size of Havasupai, along with the efficiency of ConNext, there were always redundancies built in; even though his team had seen the incident in their area, because more than one set of eyes was on things. The crash of the system likely prompted them to have another group take care of it. Everything would work out fine. So why was he scared?

Marcus was just reaching for the down button when his phone rang. He looked at the display and froze, recognizing that it was an in-system call. He knew the extension; it was his direct supervisor, Ryan. He stared at the display as it continued to ring, and then saw a green light in his peripheral vision. Without understanding why, his heart sped up. He accepted the call.

"Courson here."

"Marcus, you're not in the lab."

Marcus frowned, then cleared his throat. "No, I went up to the Centrum to help, but by the time I got there wasn't anything left for me to do." Ryan made an indistinct noise.

"That's commendable. The thing is, I need you in the lab. The outage is causing all sorts of issues. I really need someone I can trust to handle it. You know how much I value your contributions to the team."

"Thank you, sir. I appreciate you saying that."

"Good, good. Listen, it's important when we have issues with any of the systems that we all stay in our lane and make sure nothing falls through the cracks. I'm making plans based on your presence in the lab. You should be there."

Marcus stifled the urge to pull the phone away from his ear and stare at it. That made three times he'd said that. *Back in the lab.* Warning bells sounded in his head.

"I was just on my way there now. I just had to... clear my head," he said, stumbling over the words to cover up his lie. Why did he lie? Why not say he'd tried to call the cops?

"Understandable. I'll see you at the next department meeting?" Ryan said by way of goodbye, and Marcus shoved the phone back into his pocket. He pressed the button for the elevator and got on as soon as it arrived, riding down without pulling out his phone or tablet or looking up at any of the cameras.

The doors of the elevator opened, and a woman got on. She was wearing a Facilities Operations uniform and a distracted smile. He watched her push 23, then stared at the doors, trying to tamp down the sick feeling growing in his belly.

"Good morning, I hope you didn't go through the Centrum," she said, and it took him a moment to realize that she was talking to him and parse out what she'd said. She was looking at him in bemusement. He recovered quickly, turning his head to look at her and nodded.

The dropped call and the memory of the incident combined, bounced around in his head like a ping-pong ball. Without thinking, he said, "I did. It's handled. Don't worry about it, okay?" Marcus stared at her until her slightly confused expression cleared, and she nodded slightly. He resumed staring at the doors, not saying another word as the elevator soundlessly slid down.

The doors opened and he stepped into the hall, immediately colliding with Daisy. She'd set her lips in a thin, grim line, and her eyes darted everywhere, never settling. Marcus reached out with both hands to steady her and keep her from falling, keep her from spilling the contents of the box she held. He looked down and saw with some surprise the picture she kept on the shelf over her desk.

"Wait, what?" he began, but she raised her gaze to his before sliding it away, staring at a point above his shoulder.

"Hey, sorry, didn't mean to bump into you! Don't rate me too bad for it, okay?" She gave a short, harsh laugh and tossed her hair back over her shoulder, hitching the box higher in front of her to secure her grip.

"Never! You're one of my favorite people. Up votes all the way!" he said, trying to put her at ease with the old joke. Daisy gave him a dead-eyed smile and pushed past him.

"Where are you going?"

"I can't talk to you." Her voice was barely more than a whisper, but the tone was clear.

"What?" Marcus said, taken aback by her curt reply.

"I have kids! You know I have kids. I can't do this. It was nice working with you. See you around, okay?" She smiled again, looking pointedly past his shoulder at the camera. He followed her line of vision and stepped back, allowing her to pass, trying to stifle his confusion and unease.

Marcus watched her walk into an elevator and waited until the doors shut behind her before turning to walk into the lab he'd shared with his team since starting this project. A team that now obviously didn't include Daisy. He had only a moment to ponder the meaning behind her leaving, when he opened the door and saw that all three stations had new occupants.

"Hey, Marcus! So glad to finally get to work with you!" a tall, dark-haired man said, waving at him before turning back to his station with its pristine surface. Somehow, the lack of personal items made the changes feel worse. His throat closed tighter than a year-old pickle jar as panic landed like a lead weight on his chest. He'd only been gone an hour. Long enough for them to sweep his team away. Long enough for everything but his desk to change.

"Mr. Courson, I'm Oliver. Nice to meet you." Marcus nodded at the second man and turned to look at the blank-faced woman seated at the middle station.

"That's Tabitha, she'd not a talker. Hey listen, the cameras for our area of Central are still malfunctioning. How do you want me to handle it?" the dark-haired man asked, and Marcus tried to remember if he'd said his name. It didn't matter. He wouldn't let it matter. Like he'd told the woman in the elevator, it was handled. They handled everything. Managed quickly, quietly, and efficiently. He sighed and shook his head. There was nothing to do, and if he didn't pull himself together these three newbies would down-vote him out of his management position.

"Sorry, wool-gathering. I'm pretty tired today. The Centrum feed is tied to the outage. Just ignore it for the time being and get to work on the manual renormalizations. They're going to need those projections whether our feed is working or not," Marcus said, then turned and walked over to the mini fridge and pulled out a can of Coke. "Anyone want a drink? I keep it stocked for my team. Kept it, I mean... it's here for you guys, too, okay?" he said, and smiled awkwardly. The chorus of thank-yous followed him into him into his office. He closed the door and sat behind his desk.

Pulling up his duty log, he mechanically went through the motions until his chest loosened and the routine work blunted the sharp edges of his fear. Maybe he'd make time every day to go up around twilight. It wasn't as hot, and the air felt clear. He wouldn't miss things as much, or spend time worrying about things he couldn't change. Smiling at the thought, he went back to work; losing himself in the monotony until the only thing on his mind was how much he missed that bread.

16

Just Don't Look

|

I saw the first warning at the North Elevator. The yellow hazard cone with a light on top stood just to the side of the pathway, right beneath the ubiquitous *'Smiling Each Day Keeps the Down Votes Away'* poster. The cone's light was blinking, signaling official activity, and the cameras overhead flashed from red to green then back again—a subtle clue that voice recording was active. I pulled out my tablet to find the location of the issue. Of course it was on ten, right on my route.

The second warning was at the trolley stop. Another flashing yellow hazard cone next to the *'Being Seen Means Being Green!'* poster on the signpost. It said '10-minute delay'. Luckily, I could see a trolley approaching as I arrived. When it pulled to a stop I boarded, ignoring the sour expressions of the people exiting the vehicle and offering them the 'ScorCity' smile. I giggle every time I use the nickname, even in thought. It's common knowledge that ConNext uses the city and all of us as guinea pigs for their SCORE system. Thus, the nickname Score City—or ScorCity for short. Yes, I am easily amused.

I greeted the driver and the other three passengers and counted myself lucky that whatever happened had the end result of reducing the number of early morning travelers to a point that I didn't have to fight for a seat—upvotes for the driver. Of course, that placed my actions on clear view of the various cameras, but that was life in the city. Privacy was a box you clicked to indicate you understood there was none.

I reached the Centrum and began to think that maybe I should be on my guard. A uniformed guard looked at my uniform and nodded to me, I couldn't remember ever seeing guards in the park this early. I could see a line of cones adjacent to the main pathway. The first one I came upon flashed red in an incessant pulse. Every fifty feet along my normal route someone had planted a cone, its glowing tip merrily flashing to catch the attention of travelers. I could feel the hairs on my arms rising in alarm. I didn't need that. Having an anxiety attack on the way to work was not the way I wanted to start the day. I took slow deliberate breaths, syncing them to my steps to stave it off.

This was normally the most pleasant part of my commute. The ten minutes it took for me to walk through the centrum to the bridge for the elevators was the closest I got to being in nature, or outside for that matter. They said the simulated sky mirrored the sky outside, not that I'd had the time to verify that statement. They designed the forced air to mimic a light summer breeze; the openness, the wide plant-lined paths, mimicked a serene desert oasis. If not for the scent of chemicals and earth—and the smart posters with their cheery messaging on every vertical surface larger than a half-meter—it could be a park on an island somewhere. The walk never failed to relax me, but not today. Every step I took echoed in my ears, winding that ball of uncertainty tighter, so I barely noticed when a woman came running towards me, her jogging gear emblazoned with the ConNext logo. Her face was pale and flushed, and she looked vaguely familiar, but I couldn't place her.

"Did you hear? It's worse than you can imagine." I shook my head as she ran in place, using two fingers to take her pulse. "Security is still working on it. You should go another way," she continued, and I shook my head again. I had just enough time to get in and be slightly early. Any deviation would add time I didn't have.

"There isn't really another way; I'm on 23 South," I said, and saw her look at my uniform and nod.

"Just don't look." She shook her head and took off running again. This time her gait made me think of someone trying to outpace something. Some demon only she could see. I quickened my steps; the faster I passed the area, the less chance there was of seeing something that might upset me.

Not looking was impossible. Blood. There was so much of it, splattered everywhere. Shock locked my legs in place as soon as what I was seeing registered. My determination to not stare—to move past quickly—evaporated as horror took over. It took an act of will move on. Someone superstitious might have seen this as an omen. Thankfully, I'm not a superstitious person. The only thing that usually worried me was ConNext. Hopefully they wouldn't devise a whole new list of procedures because of whatever happened; we had too many as it was.

Walking past, reaching the end of the corridor, and pressing the button to go down to work took effort. My mind wouldn't let it go. I was glad that they'd removed the body already. Hoped they had. I couldn't imagine that much blood without a body would be a good thing. After all, Havasupai had 25 levels, and it was practically in the middle of nowhere. There were a lot of places to hide a body. That thought hit me like a ton of bricks and my limbs locked again.

The doors to my right slid open, but I didn't move. Couldn't move forward no matter how hard I tried. Without intending to, I backed away from the empty elevator. I couldn't do anything but feel the trembling of my limbs as my brain slid from what I'd seen to what I remembered.

It's funny how our brains work, how we hold on to things, sights, smells. How they connect us to memories. Forever linked and waiting just under the surface for some cue to spring forward and drown you with their existence. For a moment I was nine years old again, running through the woods to find someone, anyone, to help. My body wanted to rock but I ruthlessly stifled the impulse, holding myself still while my pulse raced, and my uniform grew damp with perspiration. A headache bloomed and it grounded me. With the growing pain my panic eased.

I am Delia MacPhail, the youngest female Urban Systems Engineer ever chosen for a project this large. The first woman to lead a Sustainable City project in the state, and my research is going to change the world. I am not a scared child. I am a survivor. I. Can. Do. This, I thought, and forced myself to walk forward and stab the button again as the throbbing bloom of tension started a rave in my head.

The elevator doors slid open to my left, its cabin occupied by a man who wore a uniform indicating he worked in IT. I tried to look pleasant and not relieved when his eyes slid over and past me as I entered and stood next to him, pressing 23. Then I looked up and saw the camera. Stifling a sigh, I spoke.

"Good morning; I hope you didn't go through the centrum," I said, cognizant of the flashing just above my line of vision. The sound startled him but he recovered quickly, turning his head to look at me and nodding.

"I did. It's handled. Don't worry about it, okay?" He held my gaze then looked back at the doors, not saying another word as the elevator soundlessly slid down.

When he got off six floors later I smiled and nodded, hoping that was enough to rate our interaction as positive and pulled out my tablet so I could upvote and check my list, striving to compartmentalize. I just needed to shuffle what I'd seen in. Put it in its place. I glanced up at the elevator's poster: '*We Stay Connected So You Can Too!*' then back down at my tablet. We had sixteen more days, and there would likely be changes because of what happened upstairs. Since it's my ass if my department is not operational on time, I can't afford to let that happen. Not if we want to keep control of the project. The strings had loosened a bit once ConNext stepped in but tightened in other ways, given how the company monitored things. Every action, every day.

The moment I reached Level 23 the smell hit me. I walked down the hallway, grateful for the way they'd softened the lighting and trying not to notice the stench. I'd spent the first few weeks drenched with sweat despite being so far underground. One more scent to add to the layers of awful since everyone else stunk, too. It was better now but you still noticed it, and the lights. Even when they're pleasant they're right there in the back of your mind. Hard not to obsess over light when you live your life underground.

No one was in the office when I got there, which made me happier than it should. I liked to arrive before anyone else on my team because I needed time to verify what the night crew had completed and add to the assignments for the morning shift. I also needed time to prepare myself to talk to people all fucking day. Sadly, it was a rare occurrence. It was a relief to find that, for once, the night shift had completed everything. I walked over to the wall of displays, barely glancing at them and the cheery *'Your Team Makes Life Better'* poster, before looking through the quad-pane, shatter-resistant glass that protected the control room from the plant. Green lights all around—a gleaming shrine of experimental technology. Seeing it normally left me feeling proud and satisfied, but I wasn't seeing it really. My brain was upstairs, fixating on the blood.

The whole scene had resembled something out of a horror movie, and I had to work hard to push the image away and to start working. The sound of the elevator approaching snapped me out of it and added a thin layer of steel to my will, I might still felt shaky but no one would know. Using my coping skills, I rolled my eyes and grimaced. Reminded myself that I didn't want anyone to see me fall apart. There was no reason to go to pieces; that mess upstairs had nothing to do with me, right? Taking a deep breath, I plastered the ScorCity smile on my face and looked towards the entrance. Most likely word of what happened had gotten around, spurring my team to get in on time to gossip. The odd conversations with the jogger and IT guy bothered me. Especially the man. He hadn't said much, but his expression said more. His demeanor, the aloofness, was jarring. After all, we're supposed to be nice, right? Friendly people have pleasant interactions. *We both rise when our spirits stay high* or whatever the stupid poster says.

My desk was as I'd left it, precisely organized piles of paper backups to our electronic files. Not everything, just the most important. I'd insisted on this despite the addition to my personal carbon footprint. It was my way of protecting my work. The system, when completed, would revolutionize the way humans disposed of things. The habit came from my love of science fiction. It taught me that in the event of an apocalypse, digital storage systems were the weak link in the chain. I firmly believed it would change the world, help fix what we broke. I just needed to get it working. Never mind the fact that in the event of an apocalypse, building machines to deal with refuse would be way down on the list. The point was, I didn't really trust computers; they were only as reliable as their power supply and the people programming them. Paper backups made me feel secure. Especially given the number of outages we have had in the run up to launch day.

"Doctor D! Did you see the output from the test run?" a voice called, so I rose and walked back out into the common area. My team leader was standing by the board, making notes on his pad.

"What test run? We're not scheduled for one until next week—and that's if we get the temperatures down. It's still running too hot," I said, walking over to where he stood. Jay had it right: the night crew had run the equipment during their shift.

"They used a larger sample this time. Ran it through Vat 3. Looks like it ran on spec for once. I think the adjustment you figured out made the difference." I looked at the board, confirming everything he'd just said.

"Spec would be a good start. I'll go check the tank,"

"You're going to obsess."

"It's my job. The city has to be 100% self-sustaining. That means waste reclamation and recycling have to function above spec. Once the city is full there won't be room for error." Jay rolled his eyes but didn't contradict me. I'd said the same thing so many times now he could probably quote it verbatim.

I didn't double check because I doubt them or think they lack dedication. It's just that the system is untested. Hell, every corner of the city held an experiment of some sort. Farming, waste, energy, you name it. Then on top of that there's SCORE. We are under a lot of pressure, and ConNext is recording every move we make when we're in common areas. They made sure to install and activate the cameras on this level almost from day one.

I pulled a pair of headphones off a hook on the wall next to the *'Safe-ty is an Up- V!'* poster, sliding them on before I went in. Tank Room A housed vats one through twenty-five. The vats were pristine, gleaming stainless-steel towers that reminded me of the beer tanks at my favorite brewery restaurant in Phoenix. The chutes that fed them were still, the room itself mostly quiet except for the hum of the HVAC system. The temperature controls and air purification systems on paper run silent. They are barely noticeable at ground level, but down here the roar of the machinery is clearly audible, and in the tank rooms the sound required hearing protection. Vat 3 had an additional green light, signaling run cycle completion. The tank was spotless, not even a fingerprint marred the surface, and that made me feel better. They hadn't just run the test and walked away, they'd watched and likely recorded each stage in their notes. For a moment I felt hope bloom, sure we weren't where I needed us to be, but this was a good start.

I walked down the line, checking the display panels before going back to the chute and turning it on, checking the integrity of the grates. The merry clanking of the gears as the chute activated always reminded me of the old movies with the elves in Santa's workshop, making toys and sitting them on the conveyer belt for bundling in packages with bows. There was a bit of paper stuck in the grate and I tugged it free before turning the chute off again, sliding it into my pocket for disposal later. I looked up and down the line before walking over to pull the tablet off the wall to read the outputs and notes from the test.

There weren't any.

Maybe they'd used their personal tablet for the run. Not procedure, but not the end of the world. Especially since it wasn't a scheduled test. Still, I carried the tablet back into the other room with me.

"Hey, are the notes from the test on the tablet in here?" I showed Jay the tablet from the vat room. He took it and handed me the one he held. The main lab tablet automatically logged output, but input was manual. The input field was blank.

"It was like this when you picked it up, right?" I asked, and Jay didn't bother to hide his incredulity.

"Oh sure, I just came in, picked up the tablet, and wiped half the fields in the time it took you to walk from your office," he replied, and I grimaced ruefully. He'd hardly had time to register the test before calling me to the room, let alone swipe open to the appropriate screens and wipe out half of them.

"Sorry. Of course. I guess I need to wake up Myron."

"At this hour? You're a brave woman," Jay said, and I frowned. This essentially would be the middle of the night for him, as his schedule was opposite ours. I just needed to know what they'd run through the system for their test. The rest of the numbers were there for me to use and waking Myron when he'd just gotten to sleep never resulted in anything pleasant. There was a reason he'd worked the graveyard shift his entire adult life. Thankfully, I remembered a way to get around that.

"You have a point. I'll check the camera to see if they got the sample from Facilities; if I can't figure it out then I'll call. That's probably what they did." Jay nodded in response, and I went to the server room at the back of the lab.

Like the rest of the plant, the server room was lit up like Christmas and full of gleaming tech. The city of the future sported the perfect melding of what worked from the past and what would propel us into the future. So, naturally, they'd commissioned old-fashioned servers that could act as hubs for all of their computers, with the latest tech shoehorned in to enable broadcasting wireless signals several miles underground through meters of rock. The fact that it worked at all was amazing. Even still, outages were frequent, so IT was always in and out, fiddling to boost this or replace that. And each division had its own server room complete with monitoring station—a bank of screens at the front of the room sitting on a plain metal desk with a trio of ergonomic chairs facing it. The plan eventually was to keep those stations manned as a backup to the AI ConNext provided. The theory was, keeping humans in the loop of monitoring interaction ensured that they catch any deficiencies in the software's programming. The chairs were empty, as they likely would remain. The idea that anyone would pay to have a trio of humans verify the interactions caught on each area's cameras was ridiculous and unsustainable. I had no clue what they'd end up doing to make sure that ConNext was properly logging SCORE, when the humans involved didn't bother to rate their own interactions.

I sat in the center chair and listened to the quiet hum of machinery for a moment before going down the hastily scrawled list to see which of the screens monitored the vat room in question. It was only then that I noticed that one screen was dark. My brain went back to the look on the IT tech's face, and his admonishment to not worry about it. What was it he'd said? *It's taken care of?* I frowned, trying unsuccessfully to push down my immediate horrid and paranoid thought. Because obviously the best way to dispose of a body in Havasupai would be to recycle it. Yet only an idiot would attempt to do so, as there are cameras everywhere. ConNext is always watching. Someone would know. There was no reason for me to suspect that they didn't have a body to go with that mess upstairs. Just my brain tying the past to the present and coming up with something designed to make my anxiety kick in and distract me from what mattered.

I checked the list again, knowing before I looked that the dark screen would be the one corresponding with the room in question. Waking Myron looked more likely. I swiped my finger over the interface on the desk and then asked to speak with someone in IT. It took a few minutes to get a person; the automated is default even from the in-network connections. The woman who picked up sounded stressed, not at all like the normal desperately chipper attitudes we all had adopted for work in 'ScorCity'.

"I have a camera down in one of my vat rooms. I need to pull the recordings from last night."

"Security has restricted access to all vid feeds for the next 48 hours. Everything is going through Central on 10."

"No, I'm saying the camera isn't working. I haven't tried to access it yet," I replied, and the voice cut out a bit so I couldn't hear what she said.

"Come again?" I said, and I got static then her voice came in clearer.

"I said we are not showing a camera down. Read off the location code on the monitor for me."

I read it off and she asked me to hold on. After a few minutes, the screen came on again and showed the vat room as usual.

"Your camera should be working now. Thanks for calling IT," the voice said, and I said *wait* to keep her from hanging up.

"That's not the only reason I called; I need to see the feed from last night. I just noticed it was out when I went to look."

"No one can access that remotely right now. You have to call up to Central and get them to authorize. Everything is rerouted."

"Rerouted?" I parroted, then what she'd said registered. Security had control of the cameras. It had to be the blood stains.

"Yes. So, I can't pull that for you. Thanks for calling IT," she repeated, and I didn't stop her from disconnecting. The familiar ball of worry began to roll around my stomach. Paired with the tension headache that had begun earlier, I decided to pop some pain killers. I keep them in the file cabinet in my office, so I went back in and sat at my desk, pulling open the drawer to snag the bottle. That's when I found the note written on the sticky pad just to the right of my mouse. 'Call ConNext Central.' Written in Myron's firm scrawl. I stared at the note, reading it twice while I popped the pills into my mouth and chased them with a sip of water from the bottle I kept nearby.

Given the static on the call a moment ago I decided using my phone would be better, so I dialed the main line from my cell, wading through the auto to get to a human.

"My night manager left a note telling me to call Central when I got in. This is Delia MacPhail in Facilities Ops."

"Please hold for Mr. Griffin."

I suppose hearing the name of ConNext's site rep should have worried me. It didn't. I had dealt with so much in my life, talking to the man responsible for keeping me and my team employed seemed minor. And after seeing the mess upstairs, I had enough to do just keeping my focus on my job and the things that needed doing. I only had 16 more days.

"Delia! Thanks for calling. I know you guys are super busy right now. We're only a couple of weeks away!" Ryan Griffin spoke in exclamation points. There was no other way to describe it. He pronounced every sentence as if it were part of a rousing speech some general gave on the eve of battle. In person it was bearable; over the phone, not so much.

"We're working hard to be ready."

"I know we'll be on schedule. Listen, don't worry about the hiccup last night; we will get things fixed on the back end to make sure that we don't have any more outages."

"What? I just—" I started to say, but he cut me off and barreled on.

"I know you had IT restore the cameras, so once my guy comes down to inspect it and your server, you should be good to go. I don't foresee that we will have any other hiccups."

"Well, we, umm—so you mean the outage was widespread?" I asked, not quite understanding why they'd wanted me to call personally about something that happened so frequently. I looked out my office door and through the windows at the tanks. My brain superimposed the image of the bloodstains on the grates, and for a moment I lost the thread of the sounds coming from the phone. All I could hear was my heart beating faster in a direct correlation to the growing sick feeling that the mess upstairs had somehow found its way down here.

"Several sectors last night. Unfortunately, it's playing havoc with security's ability to provide the detective what he needs to wrap this up. That's not for you to worry about. Just make sure your team keeps running tests on the equipment. We need it above spec by the ribbon cutting. Don't forget how important you are to our success! *We believe in you!*"

The line cut off. I stared at my phone for a long while, wondering what I had missed, what the point of that conversation was. The jogger's voice came back to me. I heard her say again 'Just don't look' as clearly as if she were standing in front of me. Isn't that what I normally did? That's what we did here. Why I liked it here better than back home on the surface. Havasupai kept life simple. We had all our needs met. Our teams and our neighbors were our community. We stuck together. Her warning, the tech's warning, the looks on the faces of the passengers on the trolley. People who couldn't take another route. Like me. I wasn't alone anymore. The ConNext logo meant something. Even when there wasn't a list of procedures, we understood.

It was starting to become clearer.

"Jay, call FM; I need whatever they can scrounge for us for another test. I'm thinking the outage hit at their midpoint yesterday, and that's why they lost the data," I said, walking into the common area and away from my phone and any compulsion to call Myron.

"I should have thought of that," Jay replied, and the tension I'd missed in my preoccupation cleared from his gaze.

"It's the only thing that makes sense. Time is too short to concentrate on anything but our system. We need to run above spec; in fact, tell them to go ahead and switch to Op mode. I think we're going to need to test as much as possible between now and then."

"Not give it a break between calibrations?" Jay asked but I pushed on, not willing to examine the faint hint of something in his tone.

"When we're active we won't have any breaks. We need to simulate real life," I countered, and watched him until he pulled up the required screen and sent the message. Then I looked at my watch. Decided I could get some paperwork in and then take an early lunch, be back in time for the rep's arrival. I gave Jay a small smile and nod then went back into my office and got to work. I heard the machinery kick on and looked up, watching the conveyors start moving and hearing the roar of the engines powering up before the dampeners kicked in and the sound lowered to a manageable level. Going to Op mode now would ensure we caught any issues and help us calibrate to above spec better than intermittent tests. I wrote that on my report and told myself I meant it. That this had nothing to do with the odd feeling I had after the phone call.

II

I looked at the clock and realized hours had passed without me noticing. My brain was always an interesting place. I could lose myself in my work, so this wasn't unusual. I wish I could say that I had been working, focusing on the numbers and my project, but a quick glance at my screen disproved that. It came back to the blood. Seeing it had

clicked some switch. The merry-go-round of
sound had started up, churning out its
tinkling repertoire of greatest hits. Delia
finds a body. Delia runs for help. Nothing's
left but blood. Mr. Black is missing. So is Tia
Bee. The ride is spinning faster now, and I
don't see my desk or the window into the
tank room anymore. I zoned out, not
noticing until Jay said something about
lunch to Gloria that I was sitting blank-eyed,
chewing my nail down past the quick. It was
the hint of copper in my mouth that stopped
me, knocked me free. The taste of blood from
the finger I'd mangled lost in the sea of my
mind.

I got up and went to the break room,
found the first aid kit, and took care of my
wound. Then went to my desk and opened
the drawer, pulled out my tendonitis gloves
and slipped them on, thus preventing myself
from doing it again. It was always hard
when things were so close. But that was the
way grief worked. It didn't go away; it just
took up less room until something broke the
glass on the container holding in all your
thoughts and everything spilled on the floor.
Why wouldn't it be harder to lift the things
that were heavier and put them in place

again? The clock said I had time to get lunch and get back before the rep came, so I rose, told my team I was going to grab a bite, and headed up to the food hall on 17.

Each floor above 20 had a common area like the Centrum on ten, with shops and restaurants, only without the open-air park setting. Like an old-timey strip mall just down from the elevators. The ones on 19 and 20 barely had anything. The options didn't get good until 17, which was where IT had its offices. I rarely went higher than that in search of food unless supplies were low. The higher you went, the more you found folks who liked to socialize. I knew I had to interact to some extent. It wasn't like I could forget, especially since they reminded me via my watch, tablet, phone, and the ad tickers running at eye level along every corridor wall. Oh, and the posters. Couldn't forget the posters, like the ones next to my favorite lunch stand. *'Healthy Choices Make Happy Meals'* and *'Up-V your Eats!'* They served a bowl of protein and veg over rice that had just enough flavor that you probably didn't need the dressing they offered on the side, but I always used it anyway. And the pepper sauce. I liked the spice.

I saw an empty table and took it, then began shoveling my food into my mouth to prevent having to actually speak to anyone who offered me the ScorCity smile as they passed where I sat. It was quieter than usual, something I only noticed because for once I could actually hear myself think and didn't want to. The lunch time crowd was usually boisterous and engaged, watching the streams on the screens that lined the walls of the eating areas or the tables themselves. My table played a home improvement program, though I was sure it had been showing the news when I'd sat down. It had taken me a month to acclimate to the fact that my electronics linked to the system. I preferred to watch that sort of show when I wasn't working, so of course the AI would make sure that was on when I was near a screen.

"Dr. MacPhail? Delia MacPhail?" A man in a pair of worn slacks, button-down shirt, and leather jacket stood in front of me, holding a tablet and a mug from the coffee chain stand. I nodded and continued to chew, unable to speak comfortably around the food in my mouth.

"I'm Special Agent Barron with the FBI; I'm coordinating with Mohave County PD on this case."

"You're a long way from Capital Island, Agent Barron," I replied, taking another bite of food and chewing slowly. He shrugged.

"I'm actually stationed out west, but I do answer to the guys back on the island. Given the nature of the project here, they thought it best we lend a hand. Do you have a moment to talk?"

I chewed slower, nodding my head but not making a sound.

"We're trying to get a clearer picture of the incident. While forensics is working I wanted to talk to everyone who might have seen something, given the unique camera situation you have going on here. Since your department works so closely with the facilities maintenance crew, I'd hoped you'd be able to help us piece together what happened." I swallowed and tilted my head. He was looking at me closely, too closely. As if he could see the things I hid from everyone, even myself. The rave began again, joining the soundtrack of *things to never think about* running through my head. I swayed in my seat and stopped myself, avoiding his gaze as I took a sip of my drink to soothe my suddenly dry mouth. I used my napkin to wipe my lips before replying.

"I'm sorry, Agent Barron, I don't know how I can help you, and I only get a short time to eat." I gave him the ScorCity smile and shoved another bite of food into my mouth, silently willing him to get the hint. The agent watched me chew, taking a sip of whatever was in his mug and then placed the mug on the table across from me before sitting down.

"Look, someone lost their life—surely you understand that we have to cover all the bases. I'm just looking for help," he said. I could feel his frustration, but I just stared and swallowed then lifted my fork, gesturing with it before stabbing it down into my bowl.

"This is a big city; I'm sure you'll find what you're looking for." I forked up another bite of food and put it into my mouth, this time looking past him to the camera on the wall near the entry. The one next to the *'Help is just a click away—If You See Something, Say Something'* poster. Those were almost as ubiquitous as the smiling one. Moments later a CSF officer came to the doorway and caught my eye, then moved in our direction. I tried to keep my expression blank while he stood by my table and spoke quietly in the detective's ear.

"I'm sorry, something has come up. I'll stop by 23 later okay?" he said, standing. I watched him go, continuing to eat despite my sudden loss of appetite. I put down my fork and pulled out my tablet. This was definitely a downer, I thought, wondering if they'd even bothered to set up a profile for someone who wouldn't be staying long term. They had. So rude of him to interrupt my meal, I thought, mashing my finger on the screen with a bitter smile then laughing at myself for my pettiness. He was doing his job. It wasn't his fault I didn't want to get involved. All the same, it felt like I was doing the right thing. What did I have to say, really? It had happened while I was sleeping, and handled before I'd left my home.

I saw the jogger as I rose to take my tray and the detective's cup to the sorting station. She gave me a genuine smile then turned it up to ScorCity level when she got closer. I returned her smile and nodded, locking eyes with hers when she nodded in return and readjusted her name badge before moving into the queue of users waiting to grab something for lunch. I felt again as if she wanted to tell me something but couldn't, and put it out of my mind, making the walk back to my lab and the mounds of work that waited.

FM came through in spades. When I returned the machines were churning out compost, shredded metal and gray water, and all of the conveyers were full of the detritus of the city. Overfilled, to be honest, and I watched them churn away for a moment before authorizing the team to open another room. I went over to the display and happily discovered all but one vat was running at spec. Vat 3 was running above spec. Since it was the only one adjusted along the new parameters I'd worked out the week before, that made sense. We had tons of data to analyze, and before I could blink, it was 2 o'clock and the ConNext Rep was walking through the door.

It was the Jogger. She gave me a ScorCity smile as she entered and I smiled back, somehow relieved that it was her, remembering now that we'd met twice before when the project started. I wracked my mind her for name, resorting to taking a quick peek at her nametag as she walked closer. Mayim Ehrlich.

"Mayim! Good to see you," I greeted, giving her a genuine smile in my relief.

"Delia. You as well. We have to find time once we're operational to get drinks or something so we can catch up."

"Definitely. What do you need from me?" I asked, hoping she would give me some sort of explanation for everything. Or anything. She held my gaze and her smile ramped up, never reaching her eyes.

"Oh, nothing really. I'll be out of your hair as quickly as possible. I can see you all are hard at work here." She looked into the vat room then back at me before pulling out her tablet. She typed a few words onto her screen and I read them, unable to stop myself. The words she'd typed were—*yes it did*. Then she erased them and pulled up her reports screen and typed in the date and time, walking over to the wall display and peering at it while she entered numbers on her device. I stood still for a moment, my ScorCity smile frozen on my face as the words bounced around my head without any meaning attached. I looked over at the vat room window and another piece of the puzzle clicked into place.

"Is there anything I can do to help?" I asked again, shoving my hands into my pockets because I'd felt them start to tremble.

"You all have enough to worry about. You're doing exactly what you need to do. We just want to make sure nothing like what happened last night happens again. We can't afford to lose data and have outages once the city is open and filled with non-company users. We need to be dependable."

"Up V's for dependability," I said with a forced laugh. Mayim joined in, the sound grating and overly loud.

"Make sure you save some for me, too. We need friends where we can find them down here," she said, and I nodded, trying to keep my expression the same. I looked past her, over her shoulder at the camera and its lights flickering between red and green. How often did they record sound? It didn't matter. I wouldn't let it matter. After all, I liked it here. I fit in. I had my place. Maybe I hadn't made time for friendships or relationships like other people had, but I did have people I talked to. I felt comfortable here. Mostly. I nodded and went back to my desk, looking through the window at the chutes moving their loads steadily down to the gaping maw of the vat. So efficient. My life's work. Mayim walked past me to the server room and verified the connections to all the screens and linked in with her tablet, making note of the configurations before slipping it back into the pocket of her jacket and pulling the plug on the machine. I looked down at my desk and over to the displays, verifying that everything worked. She'd clearly rerouted things through another server.

"I'm all set. I'll get out of your hair now. Let someone know if you have any issues, okay? IT is watching your other servers closely since this one had so many issues last night. We've ordered a new one that will be installed in the next few days." My eyes widened in surprise, but I didn't say anything.

"Just a precaution. We're not sure what component is off, but it clearly has a defect. Better to just replace it and move on. The clock is ticking," Mayim stated, holding my gaze. I nodded.

"Thanks for your help, Mayim. I appreciate you all responding to my issue so quickly." Her smile returned at my reply, ratcheting up past ScorCity to something sharper that warred with the relief in her eyes.

"We're always here to support you. Don't be a stranger, okay?" she said, squeezing my shoulder as she passed, walking quickly to the doors and out into the hallway.

Almost before I had time to process, the doors to the control room lab opened again—this time by the detective. He waved in my direction and I rose, walking over to stand next to him by the window.

"Detective Barron," I greeted, keeping my hands in my pockets.

He looked out into the vat room and then back at me, his mouth set in a grim line.

"If you could give me a few minutes of your time? Someplace a bit more private?" he said. I motioned for him to follow me into my office, closing the door behind him as he entered, hearing the loud squeak of the hinges from disuse.

"Have a seat, Detective, but please make this quick. As I said, I'm not sure how I can be of help here; especially given our outage last night. But I'm willing to try," I said, motioning him to the single comfortable chair in front of my desk and ramping my ScorCity smile up as far as I could without teetering into ridiculous.

"I have already been informed about the server issue, Ms. MacPhail."

"Doctor," I said, my smile remaining despite the sharpness of my tone.

"Doctor MacPhail," he corrected, and then leaned forward.

"If I could see the reports from last night? Control informed us that your night manager and Facilities Maintenance work in conjunction."

"I wish I could be of assistance there, but it just isn't possible. At least not from here."

He stared at me so long I could feel sweat starting to form under my arms. I dropped the smile and stared back, letting him see my resolve. The three words I'd read on Mayim's tablet came back to me. *Yes it did.* He wanted confirmation; I could see it on his face. It would be so easy to capitulate. Let him into our records and the vat room. Let him question my staff. I looked past him to the poster on my office wall. *'Teamwork Makes this Dream Work! The Future Depends on You!'* We were getting good results from the ramp-up. Already in the course of a few hours, I had enough data to prove that my system worked in the short run. I needed time to prove it would work in the long term. Time I wouldn't get if I let him shut things down for his investigation, if that's what he planned on doing.

What could he find? I didn't really know anything for sure, and I didn't want to know. *'Just don't look.'* The words came back to me and I widened my eyes, trying to stave off the panic I began to feel. What if I wasn't just being paranoid and letting my issues color this situation? What if there really was something for him to find and I was standing in the way of it? Did he know about me?

Did he know about me?

Did he know that I'd found a body once? Found it and the splatters and puddles that proved my friend Tia had died hard and horribly. Had led them back to where the body was, only to have them find nothing but a very few blood stains. Just enough to lend credence to the fact that I had seen something. But not enough to prove anything. And they'd never found her. They'd found Mr. Black. Days later his bullet-ridden body turned up in the woods behind Tia's house. Tia's father had gone to jail for it. They'd found him. But not Tia. No closure for the family. No funeral or memorial. No one believed me. He probably knew. It was in my psychological profile, the one they'd made us take before finalizing our hiring contracts. My history of instability due to childhood trauma, the thing that drove me and made me the reliable, quiet person I am today. I'd learned the hard way to keep my mouth shut. He had to know that when pushed I would push back. Staring and intimidation meant nothing to me. I had a deadline, and he was in the way.

"You have to know that we just want to make sure we know everything there is to know about the accident," he said, and I nodded, waiting for him to continue. When he didn't, I spoke up.

"If there was something I could do, some bit of information I had, I would tell you," I said, and it wasn't really a lie. I didn't know for sure that they'd dealt with things upstairs down here, in Vat 3. But I didn't have to know. The design of my machines assured that even if I let him go over everything, chances were there wasn't anything to find. My work is that good. I could dispose of a thousand bodies and no one would be able to tell from the output what had gone into creating it.

The merry-go-round started again, the sound mocking me, mocking the lies I told myself to justify my noncooperation. Is that part of what ConNext wanted, or just me? Did it matter?

When he left, Jay and Gloria exchanged conspiratorial smiles with me and winked. I shrugged and gave the thumbs down sign before picking up the tablet on the wall to get back to work. For some reason, in that instant I remembered the piece of paper in my pocket. I walked back into my office and stood in the one blind spot to the right of the door, pulling it out to look at it before throwing it away.

There was a word written on the paper. 'Shanna'. I turned the torn bit over to see what, if anything, was on the back, but didn't find anything. I put the paper back into my pocket and shook my head, my gaze moving around the room and landing on the poster. Mayim's voice echoed in my ears: *"Just don't look."*

17

Moving On

"Arizona is hotter now, but we'll be fine in the city. Don't think it will ever get as bad as it was back in '28, when they had the fire whirls in the wildfires. Ever seen a fire whirl?" Gerald stood on his deck, looking out in the direction of the ocean. They'd bought the house for the view almost 18 years ago, not thinking about what time would do to the land around them.

"What's that?" his daughter Monica asked, walking up to stand beside him. She still held the brochure, the glossy laminated paper with the ConNext logo on the bottom right corner of the front over the gorgeous sunrise photo of the entrance to the 'City of the Future'.

"It's a tornado made of fire. Spins through the land in a whirlwind of death. Sucks the trees right out of the ground as it burns them. Not that there's many left out there—trees that is."

"Like those funny old shark movies?" she asked. He thought for a moment then nodded, a wry smile on his lips.

"Yeah, only real. I stood fifty feet from one. Hell, they had videos of them on the news before the governor pulled the plug on them to keep folks from panicking."

"What do fire whirls have to do with this?" she asked, and he shook his head.

"I'm getting there. I saw a lot of the state before I retired. You know I first went as part of the team on the ground to fight the wildfires back in '28. Not too many of us made it out alive." She nodded, remembering her mother and siblings talking about the months of fear and anxiety they'd suffered while her father was helping save what they could in the face of so much destruction.

"Yet you want to go back." He shrugged, looking out over the horizon, his eyes on the setting sun.

"I don't fight fires anymore. I build things. But I know fire. Floods from these new walls and mudslides that wipe the land clean—I don't like those, can't understand them. No real way to stop a wall of water or mud. You got to pick your battles. I want to pick one I know how to win. Besides, there's nothing for us here anymore."

"There's not that much water here," she countered, and he shook his head.

"Pretty soon there'll be nothing but water here—salt water. The coast is more dangerous than the desert at this point. And you get SCORE for moving. Enough to bump us back up and into the next level." He sighed, knowing that's what it boiled down to. Things changed, SCORE mattered. Everything you did when anyone could see you counted now.

"What about the rumors? About the accidents and ConNext?"

"That was five years ago. ConNext has made major changes since then. You know the first version of anything is buggy."

"And the accidents?"

"There wasn't any proof they were anything but. Any project that large is going to have glitches. Seems like they worked them out, otherwise there wouldn't be the push to get more residents." He shrugged again.

"It's because of me, isn't it? Because they caught me at the protest." She looked at him and he didn't quite meet her eyes.

"It's not against the law to protest," he hedged, turning to look out over the railing again.

"Still."

"We only moved to California because your brother was going to school here. You're already looking to go to college in Arizona. Makes sense for us to move."

"I haven't been accepted yet. I don't finish high school for another year." He looked at her again, their late-life baby. Their oldest, Gavin, had been 18, and Lila 15 when his wife announced she was pregnant. The move from Texas made sense at the time. Gavin's acceptance to UCSB, and Texas' slow slide from conservative extremism to outright lunacy made the decision easy. He'd interviewed with the California Wildland Fire Hand Crew and took the first offer they made.

"Even if you're not, there're a lot of schools in the state. A lot of opportunities that will open once we level up."

"I don't care about SCORE."

"Don't say that, Monica. Think it if you must, but don't say it. Not when you're around me, around anyone."

"It's the reason things are getting worse, Dad. People are petty. Self-serving. Every morning when you wake up you find out just how few friends you have and how much worse it can be."

He looked at her again, then back at the setting sun. He couldn't deny it. Wouldn't bother trying to justify the odd shift in their society. He'd been born in 1981. Watched the rise of personal computers and the disappearance of the old ways of doing things. So much from his childhood only existed in museums now. Pay phones, radios, free television. Now he had a watch that monitored his vital signs, and carried a phone in his pocket that he used for everything. Even his job fighting fires had used robots in the end—something he'd only seen in old science fiction movies growing up.

Times had changed. The one constant for his generation especially was change; they'd cut their teeth on it, become used to it. Used to the hard sprint of progress lapping the dinosaurs of the past. Some might consider him a dinosaur, too. Yet he'd rolled with the punches and changed, too; he'd had to. Now his body couldn't do field work anymore. So he had to find new ways to make a living and contribute to society. This new society where everyone had a part to play. Everything about it was extreme, yet he couldn't even say he hadn't seen it coming. Maybe he hadn't understood how anyone could make money off of it, but the concept—that was only a matter of time.

"You're right. People can be petty. As soon as the internet gave folks a means to share their opinions on any and everything, it was inevitable they would use it as a means to feel more powerful. To win. Who doesn't like winning?"

"It sucks."

He agreed with that, too. What had they become? Clicking boxes, liking, and sharing. Taking that small step from rating a restaurant to rating a person. Rating a friend. Once you added the need to move away from traditional currency to the mix, you got where they were now. Social credit—trading behaviors for points in a system designed to keep things moving along smoothly. Not fairly. Not happily. Smoothly. Everyone knew it wasn't fair to push folks like him out of the city and away because they disagreed with enacting a kind of climate apartheid. But it kept ball rolling along its track.

"SCORE is like a wildfire, hon. It's a fact of life in our society now. Something to respect, to manage. Something like a fire whirl. You don't try to stand in the way of it, or you'll get burned and swept away." He pointed to the brochure she held and continued.

"This can be a new future for us, someplace where things aren't tilted so heavily to one side. Most of the world isn't binary. Not all one thing or another. And the future isn't black and white. Those protests you were a part of—the heart of them isn't either. Life is shades of gray. I'm proud of you for standing up for what you believe in. Proud of you for trying."

"But you want us to move," Monica said, looking down at the brochure and curling her lip. Earth-sheltered city of the future. A cave. That's what it was, no matter how nicely you tricked it out. It was still a cave. Living like moles underground, only coming up when forced. Because everything you needed was there, right?

"We have a choice to make. I want you to get on board with this. It's just the two of us now—your brother moved there two years ago, and your mom is gone." He closed his eyes, turning back to look at the slowly sinking sun. The pain hadn't dulled yet, and probably never would. "Your sister isn't moving back from D.C. She's going to marry her partner; I could tell when they visited. The high school there is top-rated, and you'll be a part of the first graduating class. Then you can decide where you want to go for college in the state, and have a home someplace that doesn't have to worry about the temperatures rising."

"No need to protest when you live in such a cool place, right Dad? I can just be a quiet, well-behaved senior locked in an underground city so I don't bug the rich folks out here anymore," Monica snapped. Gerald sighed, shaking his head.

"You can protest in other ways. Once we're there, once we're safe and have recovered from the SCORE dip." He faced her, holding her gaze with his own. "The time is coming quickly where your level color is going to be what matters, anyone with a brain can see it. This makes sense for us. I would rather you came willingly and looked at this like an adventure. Not a punishment."

Monica stared back at him then sighed, turning to face the railing and the last rays of sunset.

"I'll miss this. We've never lived anywhere else." Gerald reached out and put an arm around her shoulder, pulling her closer so they could watch the sunset together. The sky burned in shades of orange, red, and purple, hovering over the edge of the water like a fire whirl of color sweeping the world towards night. His daughter took her eyes off the horizon for a moment to pull out her phone and take a selfie of the two of them together and then quirked her lip and swiped over to up-vote her dad. He returned her smirk and hugged her closer, shaking his head as the sun continued to slide out of sight.

"I will, too," he said, giving her arm a squeeze. "I will, too."

18

A Bucket of Hope

"All of it. Into the box. Even the jewelry," Delia said the moment I entered her home. It was an odd way to start a conspiracy but I complied, silently stuffing my purse, phone, and tablet into the large metal box on the low shelf by the door. She stood beside me, swaying slightly on stockinged feet, waiting as I divested myself of anything that might harbor a microchip. Trying not to goggle, I quickly removed my rings and necklace, then toed off my shoes after realizing she was staring at my feet in expectation. The foyer was like something out of a museum. No holo-pad by the door, no screen on the wall. No holo-emitters or tablets recessed in the shelf or table. Then there was the woman herself. Delia's dark hair was long and slightly bushy, pulled back in a frayed braid that looked like she hadn't remembered it existed today. Her clothing was expensive, but unkempt and mismatched. If I squinted, I could see the resemblance to the professional photos I'd seen of her, with her hair and makeup applied by people paid to make you look perfect.

Following her from the foyer through an enormous set of double doors, I took the seat across from her in the living room and regarded my host silently. Delia MacPhail was living proof that you could tell when someone has lived through things that scarred them. It threw me off but shouldn't have, since no one knew much about her before she started working for ConNext. Clearly, there was something. The evidence was sitting before me. It was her eyes mainly, but there were other signs. Like the way her hands shook with a fine tremor and the way her gaze shifted and never settled on me as she lifted a carved bamboo bowl to her lips to take a long draw, filling the room with smoke.

Parallel: A Collection Of Science Fiction Short Stories

I'd prepared for this every way I could think of. Following and up-voting the right people. Commenting on the popular things. Getting enough credit to travel and setting up an alibi that was hard to disprove since 99% of it was the truth. I opened my mouth to speak, then closed it again. I had no clue what to say.

Delia's home was dark despite the early morning sun that baked the surrounding land. We were in for another triple-digit day. Back home, the weather was more reasonable this time of year. Thankfully, after I finished with her, I could leave. Staying in the South, where so much was dying or dead, made little sense to me. Neither did living in archaic adobe and wood structures above ground. Sadly, some people didn't like change, even if the change was good. After a long, awkward silence, I cleared my throat and spoke.

"Thanks so much for agreeing to see me," I said, and she finally looked at me. I wished she hadn't. Her eyes. I knew she was relatively young, somewhere in her late 40s, but her eyes added years. Aged her. Seeing them, I questioned the plan and my instructions to gain her cooperation.

"Well, Christina, since you're not a reporter, and you've jumped through the hoops to get to me, it's the least I can do." Delia shrugged and lifted the pipe again, releasing me from her gaze to stare out the one uncovered window. The house had a lot of windows. More than seemed wise in Arizona, with the climate being what it was. She'd angled each of the six chairs in the large square room to face a window so that, no matter where you sat, you could see out into the open land beyond. Delia frowned and sat quietly as I fidgeted a bit, trying to figure out how to continue the conversation.

"Still, I appreciate it. I know you're a busy woman," I said, for lack of anything better.

"Overseeing revolutionary technology five miles underground, where no one sees or cares." She laughed bitterly and placed the pipe back into her mouth, but didn't draw on it—instead, worrying the end with her teeth as she settled herself deeper into the overstuffed chair.

"That's not true. It's amazing, really. Groundbreaking. Your system is in all of our textbooks now, after only 15 years. You are an icon. That's why I wanted to interview you, get your help to get my classmates in to tour. We wanted someone who knows it, who lives in Havasupai and could tell us where to go and what to do. Who better than the creator?" I said, and she made a derisive noise, plainly scoffing at the notion.

"An icon? More like a useful steppingstone. Since so many people used my work as a springboard, it relegates my contributions to the footnotes. Anyway, this is my home now. I haven't lived there for more than a year. Fact is, I only go back to work. No. That's not it. You want to talk to me for the same reason everyone else wants to talk to me. You're just smarter." She pinned me with her gaze again, and I tried not to squirm.

"I don't deny having a bit of morbid curiosity. But that's not why I'm here."

"You want to repeat that lie about the class, when there's a virtual tour of the system online? One that's been there since before the first residents moved in." She pulled the pipe out of her mouth and used it to point at me as she said this. I tried not to wince.

"The online tour isn't—" I began, and she cut me off.

"No. You have another reason for being here," she said, then clamped her mouth shut so abruptly it was like she swallowed the rest of her sentence, her lips trembling with the force of the action. Then she tilted her head and stared out the window, lost in thought. The silence went on for so long that I wondered if she'd fallen asleep with her eyes open, like a cat or an old person. The idea set my nerves on edge. When she started speaking again, it startled me.

"You want something. Want it badly enough that you came down to Arizona and braved our soft triple-digit spring weather to visit the mad engineer who lives above ground in the middle of the desert." She nodded, and began puffing at the pipe again. I chewed my lip, wondering what to say since she clearly had no interest in cooperating.

"That's true, but I'm not trying to upset you or make trouble."

"Really? Knowing who I am and who I work for? I like my life," Delia said, and I stifled the urge to call her on the lie. No one could live happily like this.

"I apologize if my coming makes things difficult," I said instead, with a tight smile.

"I won't have difficulty unless you go get petty on the app. I'll know in the morning, since you're the only person I'm seeing today," she said, and gave me a look that made me squirm a bit. Seventeen hours left until Zero Hour, and she wouldn't see anyone? Wouldn't have any other interactions to rate that changes her score when everything reset at midnight? If anyone else said that, I would call them a liar. This time I believed it. She didn't seem like good company.

In the 20 years since the country's full implementation of the social credit system—SCORE—who you saw and what you did became more important than money. Living alone was a sure way to make sure you never got enough SCORE to do anything more than just subsist.

"I would think your band is high enough that any pettiness on my part would hurt me more than you," I said before I could stop myself, and Delia smirked.

"Heard that, did you? Yeah, I got a nice boost for my work. Not that it matters. I have everything I need here." She shrugged, and I looked around the room with its odd arrangement of chairs. There were no other furnishings aside from the small wooden tables between them, and no electronics or decorations of any kind.

"Why'd you agree to see me, then?" I asked, and she shrugged.

"Havasupai is a small city. We rarely get people clamoring to talk to anyone in my department. Trash isn't sexy. Yet in the past six weeks, college students have approached three of us from the same area. I was curious."

"And no one else was?"

"None of the others are anywhere near blue," she retorted, and I couldn't argue. Given her SCORE band, she could get away with a lot more than I could at Green. Not as much as Violets or Ultraviolets, but Delia was Indigo. It would take a lot to dip her SCORE enough to change the way she lived.

"I am glad you were curious enough to accept," I said, and she frowned.

"Spit it out. If I like your reason, maybe I will tell you the story as a reward. Maybe not. I don't enjoy thinking about it. If I think about it too much, the dreams start." Delia shook her head, and I decided against prevarication. Everything they'd told me let me think that, even if she said no, she'd keep her mouth shut about this conversation. I had little to fear in laying my cards on the table.

"We want your help. They felt I was the best person to ask because, well, I wasn't lying about my major and all that. So, they thought you might speak to me since we have that in common," I said, trying not to sound uncertain or scared.

Delia raised one thin eyebrow. I had the feeling I'd surprised her.

"Well now, and just who would 'we' be? I can probably guess. You're young enough to think you can change things. Young enough to believe you can make a difference down so deep, it'll take something strong to shake it free. Activists of some sort." She smiled then—a hard, biting smile. I had the feeling she could see my thoughts if I'd had any. I almost looked down at myself to make sure I was wearing clothes, her smile was that canny. Like she saw everything I'd thought, believed and done, and found it lacking.

"I remember when I was like that. Not when I was a child, but later. I had hope. I was on fire to change the world. Took hard work and hard knocks before I lost it. I learned some things just aren't possible. That you can't win some battles."

"I don't believe that," I countered, and she gave me another brittle smile.

"You wouldn't. Not yet. Give it time. Meanwhile, why don't you tell me what you want from me?" Delia said, and I shook my head.

She stood, walking to the window directly in front of her to close the curtain and then open the ones on the window next to it, following the sun. I watched her, biting my lip to keep from asking if the reason she lived like this was because of Havasupai and knowing we hadn't come to near any type of meeting of minds that would allow for such a presumptive question. Havasupai, a canyon and caves turned into the largest earth-sheltered city ever built in the United States. Deep enough that the fact that you could no longer walk on the surface for nine months out of the year didn't matter.

"You said you wanted me to join you. Join what? What makes you think I would stand with you, when I don't even stand for myself?" Delia said, staring out the window before turning to move back to her chair. She plopped down and used her lighter to ignite the bowl of her pipe again, taking a big draw of the herbal blend and holding it in for a long count before blowing out the smoke in one long, hissing breath.

"Because we think you want what we want. Deep down. You're still here working for them, but you're still you. That's the one thing all the articles and streams say every time. You're the only one who has lasted. Even within the company, you're an enigma," I said. Delia looked at me sharply, her eyes holding mine for a long, uncomfortable beat.

"You're going after ConNext."

I didn't reply, but she could see the answer on my face. Normally, just saying that out loud was trouble, but the absence of electronics loosened my tongue.

I pursed my lips, unsure how to answer her, letting the silence drag out a bit. ConNext. First social media startup, now Big Brother's right hand.

"I'm right, aren't I? You're asking my help to go after ConNext. You want me to risk my position, my life, to help take down my employers when you clearly have no clue what is really going on. Your 'we' is going to get you into trouble," Delia said finally, and shook her head sadly.

"I know what's going on," I said.

"Not if you're going after ConNext, you don't."

She stared at me for a long moment. I had the feeling she was fighting some internal battle that my presence instigated. She leaned forward, her brow furrowed, and clenched and unclenched her hands on the pipe.

"You think you can survive what will hit you if you get caught doing this, whatever this is?"

"It needs to be done," I said, and she shook her head.

"Lots of things need doing. Doesn't mean you should." She sighed. "You strike me as smarter than this. Your email led me to believe you were."

"I'm smart enough to know when to take a stand for what I believe in."

"You should be smart enough to know when to sit down," Delia said, and shook her head again.

"You want to know why I live the way I do?" she asked softly, and I stared, unsure if I should interrupt now that her posture had changed from accusatory to sympathetic. And she was sympathetic. I could see it in the way her haunted eyes welled with moisture and the sudden tension in her posture. As if the idea of me—of us trying to take on the monolith that is ConNext with their government backing and contracts and ubiquitous dealings with companies big and small—had struck some chord in her.

"I live like this so I can choose when I am seen." She put the pipe down on the table next to her. I was glad. My head felt fuzzy from being so close to her while she puffed away on her high-class joint.

"You don't get Havasupai the evolution of things. Living there, in the beginning, it was like being in a fishbowl. Where the owner is a sadistic little shit who occasionally uses his thumb to press you into the bottom to see what your fins feel like when they beat against his skin. It's not much better now." She leaned back and crossed her legs, clearly relaxed now that the herb kicked in.

"You ever read the book *1984*?" she asked, and I shook my head.

"No, I can't say that I have. I've heard of it, of course," I said, and she nodded.

"Everyone has heard of it, but they don't make you read it in school anymore. Don't want folks thinking too hard about the similarities. Cause things are so great now, right?" I nodded, but she didn't seem to notice.

"They ran things like a parody of that damn book. ConNext as Big Brother, only tongue-in-cheek 'cause they're not bad guys, right? They're always watching. Listening even until you were afraid to take a shit for fear of someone remarking on how many squares of toilet paper you used. Rewarding folks for scoring everything they see." She shook her head. "That was them learning how to make this all work. And you want to take them down. You don't even understand how they operate."

"Everyone knows how they operate. The entire country has a SCORE now, don't they?" I said, and she smirked.

"Yes, and most of the other countries have their own social credit system, too. That doesn't mean that you or anyone else knows jack shit about how and why they do what they do."

"I didn't come here to argue with you," I said, and she scoffed.

"No, you just came here full of newfound activism, determined to do your part to end tyranny by convincing the lead engineer of the company's flagship city to toss off her shackles and join your cause."

"You haven't even heard the plan."

"One made by someone outside of the company, outside of the city. It has a snowball's chance in hell of working."

"That's why we need you," I said, and she sucked her teeth in disgust.

"Right. Great. Except—" Delia shook her head, "you're fighting the wrong enemy."

"ConNext is not the wrong enemy. SCORE is evil," I said, not understanding how everyone—how I—could have read her so wrong. It seemed impossible that someone like her would be on their side.

"I agree. But likely for a different reason," she replied, interrupting my thought. I looked at my hands, trying to figure out what to say.

Delia picked up the bamboo pipe and reached into her pocket, pulling out a leather pouch and filling the bowl with a generous pinch of dried leaves. Meticulously packing it in, she replaced the pouch before lighting the pipe and sucking the smoke deep.

"Medicinal. But the effects don't last long. Especially when I have to think about this."

"I don't want to trigger you," I said, and she laughed. The sound was hollow, mocking the idea that I could be so important.

"I don't need any help with that. The noise from this shit is just the latest in a lifetime of horrors on my mind's merry-go-round of sound," she said, and shook her head again, looking past me to stare out the window.

"You going to tell me what happened?" I prompted, and she shook her head.

"No, it's just more noise. You'll repeat it and it will become just another theory. So many stupid theories. It's always the same. Every time anything happens, everyone says something and someone believes it. That's the issue, you see. This wasn't the first incident, just the first that definitely didn't fit into the near-miss category, and we treated it like everything else."

I opened my mouth to contradict her, then reconsidered. She was right. Even outside of her city, above ground, wasn't that how the world worked now? Even with video evidence and eyewitnesses, someone makes up a version of the tale in the retelling, and that version becomes a new truth to compete with the facts. She looked at me and smiled grimly.

"So, there are other incidents we don't know about," I said, quietly latching on to the other important piece of information she'd dropped.

"You're quick. Maybe you'll figure it out before you leave here." She put the pipe down again and leaned forward.

"What do you mean?"

"I did my research. You remind me of myself. Well, myself without the issues. That's partly why I agreed to meet you."

I shook my head, vaguely insulted. Insult melded with disappointment that bounced around in my gut and made it hard to sit still and listen to her. I couldn't reconcile the Dr. Delia MacPhail of the books and streams with the bitter, distracted woman sitting before me. The Delia in the books would have listened to my pitch and jumped at the chance to fight back against injustice and take back privacy. This rambling woman, in her barely furnished box in the middle of the desert, puffing away at a pipe that likely cost as much as my college tuition, was no one's hero. She didn't look stable enough to run anything. Yet she did. Her tenure as the head engineer in Havasupai had won her tons of accolades, writeups, and a permanent place in the textbooks used by current Urban Systems Engineering majors, myself included.

"I didn't lie in my letter. I've looked up to you ever since I learned your name. What you've done makes life better. It goes a long way towards fixing everything we broke," I said, reminding myself of who she was and who she was to me. I struggled to let go of my expectations. Delia nodded after a moment and then continued.

"I believe you, I do. In fact, I think I'll tell you about it after all," she replied, then used that pipe to point at me again. "You have spunk. You wouldn't have lost it the way I did after I saw the mess that day. I barely made it to the elevator bank before I fell apart. Had to work to pull myself together, press the button, and get on an elevator. Fact is, if it hadn't been for the odd conversation with the guy in the elevator going down, I probably would have turned around and gone home. The long way." She shook her head.

"You said you had a weird conversation?" I said, prodding her to elaborate.

"Several. That's the thing. We all knew, see? Knew someone was always watching. Even when they claimed they weren't. The guy in the elevator, the security guard who rescued me from having to talk to the detective about what I knew—everyone. ConNext didn't tell us what to do or say. No one told me to down-vote my conversation with the detective. No one in ConNext said anything that forced any of us to keep our mouths shut and mind on our own business. They didn't have to."

"Out of fear?" I asked, and she shrugged.

"Fear, conditioning, selfishness, myopia. Whatever. Our livelihoods depended on the project's success, on the city's success. The death of one reporter was small potatoes compared to the money and futures on the line for everyone involved."

"How did she die?" I asked quietly. Delia stared out the window for a long moment, her hands shaking in her lap as she turned the pipe around in circles absently.

"Does it matter?"

"Of course it matters," I said, furrowing my brow in confusion.

"Why?"

"Because… someone died? I mean, it matters who killed her. It matters what happened to her body. That's why there're so many rumors. Because no one knows!" I threw my hands up in frustration. "ConNext did that! Her family got a check, but they had to promise not to sue—or talk."

"ConNext did not *DO* anything," Delia said and stood, walking to the window to look out again. "The people who needed to know what happened, know what happened. The rumors. That's on us like everything else," she said, and I shook my head.

"It's on ConNext. They made the world like this," I said, trying to get through to her.

"No. People made the world like this. We did it. We wanted robots and machines to make things easier for us, so we had more time to devote to things other than basic survival. We wanted a way to punish businesses and people in the service industry who don't give us the respect we feel we deserve. We wanted people to pay attention to us and think we're smart or funny or important. We wanted proof in some tangible form that we're not just tiny parasites crawling on the face of a spinning rock in the corner of an insignificant galaxy bobbing towards annihilation with the rest of the universe." She walked closer as she said this, her eyes swimming with some emotion I couldn't pinpoint.

I stared back, turning what she was saying over in my head.

"So we shouldn't care, because we're all going to die? I didn't take you for a nihilist. Your work, the ability to reclaim materials and break them down into usable components in a quick, safe, carbon neutral way—that screams hope. It's a solution that is already helping us fix things. That doesn't seem compatible with what you just said," I retorted, and she shook her head, moving back to her chair.

"That's because you're not listening. I never said we shouldn't care, just asked you if it mattered. I asked because even if I tell you the truth, you need to see that ConNext isn't the issue. Taking them down, telling the world how bad their system is, won't fix things."

"SCORE is the problem. Why can't you see that? SCORE is the reason they could cover up the murder," I said, and Delia shook her head.

"There wasn't a murder. She died. No one killed her. At least not on purpose. It really was an accident."

Her voice was quiet as she said this. She put her pipe in her mouth and puffed on it while I sat floundering, mouth agape.

"But her body," I said, and Delia shook her head.

"Incompetence. Negligence and overwork. Optimizing systems to remove as many humans as possible to cut back on the number of people you have to pay has consequences. Shit happens."

"Death isn't just shit happening," I retorted.

"Sometimes shit is horrible. We live in a society where horrible shit happens daily. Hourly, even. And we ignore it because it isn't convenient. We down-vote folks who mention it and spoil the mood."

"You see it, then. You said it. We down-vote folks who mention it. SCORE does that. It makes people callous and myopic."

"Does it? You think people weren't like this before SCORE?" she said, and shook her head. "Okay. Fine. Say I agree with you. Tell me what you want. I can see that you don't understand. Maybe you will one day, but for now." She shrugged, and the confusion I felt turned to hope despite the oddity of the conversation up to this point.

"You agree with me, then you'll help. We just need another person on the inside to help facilitate when the queen makes her move."

Delia's laugh was full-bellied and pushed back the hope I felt. My cheeks heated as anger and confusion battled for supremacy, leaving me unmoored, buffeted by the waves of her amusement.

"You already have someone inside? What more do you need than a single person with access to the system? What you want proof they're evil, too? Why don't I just give you a copy of the recording of the vacuum grinding Shannon's body into pieces so it could suck her up? It will be faster and have the same effect as anything any of your operatives can do. None. No one cares. No one cared then, and no one will care now. It won't bring them down. Even if it had a chance of working and did everything you wanted it to, someone else would step in and fill the same niche ConNext holds now," she said, and horror had me leaning back in my chair as if to escape the brutality of the statement.

"A video of—you mean to say that's how she died and there's a video of it?"

"What? No. She was dead before that. The robot vacuum didn't kill her. This isn't some weird dystopian world where robots rise and eat their makers. Well, okay. You could make an argument about the dystopian part." She shrugged again.

"But why?" I began, and she waved a hand, silencing me.

"No. I'm not telling you anything else. You can make up your own version to fit the facts I just gave you. You want to bring down SCORE, right? End the way we rate each other based on how we feel our interaction went. You want to tear down the system and, what? Take things back to the way they were when we reserved ratings for restaurants and other businesses, or kept our thoughts about our neighbors to ourselves? You think exposing ConNext as some sort of bogeyman that has changed the way we treat each other or breaking their servers or something will make people stop caring about the points?" Delia shook her head sadly.

"We have to do something. We can't just accept that this is the way things are."

"Why not? Nothing lasts forever," she replied. And this time I shook my head, denying what I didn't know.

"We have to try. It's the fight that gives us hope for all the tomorrows," I said, and she smiled, another genuine one.

"Exactly. But you can't talk about hope like it's magic. Hope isn't a bird. It isn't some fragile, flighty thing floating through the air like inspiration feeding your soul. Hope is the plug at the bottom of an old bucket. Sealing the hole and keeping all your dreams inside. It's slimy and worn and occasionally leaks from wear and tear. It gives us the strength we need to survive—to try," she said, and I nodded, finally seeing the woman I'd read about in the quiet words.

"I want to keep trying. But I need your help. We need your help," I said, and she sighed and nodded, then stood and moved across the room to the door.

"I'll do what you want, on one condition. Maybe it will help me sleep. Help me feel better about standing back to watch while they covered up the results of their micromanaging and incompetence by throwing money and SCORE at everyone involved," Delia said. I stood and followed her as she walked towards the entrance, our audience clearly at an end.

"What's the condition?" I asked as she reached to open the double doors that led from her living room to the small foyer where I'd left my things.

"When this fails, you sit down and think about what the real problem is. Then call me and talk to me about how we fix that."

Parallel: A Collection Of Science Fiction Short Stories

19

Zeroed Out

"Have you seen the new intern?"

The trio of DMSs looked up when Dr. Lea Zelenskyy entered the room. The specialists wore the sleek ConNext logo polos and slacks but still looked unkempt next to Lea in her tailored suit and monogrammed lab coat, and she'd had to wade through the mob at the gates to get there. All the DMSE[1]s wore lab coats, as if they were medical doctors instead of PhDs. ConNext insisted, which sometimes made the computer lab feel like a clinic when a group of them were in there together.

---

[1] Data Mining Systems Engineer

"I sent him to get the ZH error log reports hard copies because we're not sure what's causing our problem."

"What problem?" Lea asked and again the others looked at the one who'd spoken before, clearly designating him as the official bearer of bad news. They had buried her in bureaucracy as soon as she'd arrived, so she hadn't noticed that anything was wrong. She looked around, noticing for the first time the odd silence. The room was empty aside from these three. Not normal at all for 10 AM.

"Well, it's just that it's looking like we didn't Zero last night. When we came in, half of the computers up here—the ones hooked into the main server—displayed an error code. The other half are full BSOD. We can't address it until we can tell JC where to look," The senior-most analyst said, and the other two nodded, reminding Lea of the old bobble head toys she'd had as a child.

"How long ago was that?" she asked, looking at her watch. She had just enough time to grab a cup of coffee before heading up to meet with that prick, Gressmann. She needed his okay for the last addition to the Canadian deal. But if they hadn't Zeroed, there was no way she'd get the coffee or make the meeting on time.

"Not long, he—um, well actually he should have been back by now. Want me to go—" Lea cut him off with a wave of her hand and left the room, striding quickly to the elevators and taking them down to level zero—or the hub as they liked to call the main server complex around the sealed chamber that housed the quantum computer. With any luck, she could troubleshoot the issue and round up the intern. Two birds with one stone.

Trekking past the security post and decontamination rooms, she looked ahead and saw the sealed chamber that housed the Quantum Computer. The thick glass window and concrete walls muted the hum to something less than audible but still prevalent. Inside the hub antechamber a lone figure sat at one of the trio of desks, his gaze fixed on the paper in his hand. Lea cleared her throat.

"Malcolm, isn't it? I am Dr. Zelenskyy. You were supposed to meet with me today about your reassignment."

The young man looked up and flushed with what looked to be a combination of embarrassment and fear. He scrambled out of the chair, knocking it backward so it rolled a few feet away and spun in place.

"Oh! Ms.—I mean Doctor Zelenskyy. I lost track of the time. The guys sent me to get the ZH printout because of the error...you know the error? But when I got down here and looked at the paper I got confused, so I was going over the logs."

Lea mentally counted to ten, then replied.

"What confused you?"

"The error. Someone named JC has been doing some Cowboy Coding to get around it. Keeps spitting out dates, figures, then after a short compile goes back to this."

Malcolm held up the paper so she could see the lines of code ending with

: [//// reset_0X00000EF////

Lea looked at the paper, then picked up a second page and scanned it quickly. Almost identical.

"You said JC has been writing the code?"

"Yeah, renormalization subroutine. This guy is amazing, never seen anything like it, but I guess it's because of the Quantum Computer, right? I don't have much experience with them."

"Well, that's what you are here for," Lea said absently, examining the pages in her hand. She looked up at the intern again.

"Did you ask the computer what it meant?"

"What do you mean, ask the computer?" Malcolm said, and Lea shook her head.

"We have a voice interface. Listen, head on upstairs and tell the guys to pull the logs for the past month. I'll stay here and wait for them to print."

Lea sighed. He was so young. And so many of the interns barely did any research before they applied. She felt ridiculous standing in the basement waiting for paper from a printer in 2122. There were probably twenty printers in the entire complex. Printing things was an obsolete practice. But occasionally it helped them to better visualize problems. Since the hub was a closed system to protect the Quantum Computer from intrusions, if you wanted access to it you had to physically go access it. She walked over to the large wall display next to the window overlooking the computer room.

"Computer, activate voice interface."

"VOICE INTERFACE ACTIVE. GOOD MORNING, LEA."

Lea frowned. That's a first.

"Good morning. Please provide a daily score overview report."

"SPECIFY DATE."

"Yesterday, April 17, 2122."

"THERE ARE NO FILES MATCHING THAT DATE."

Lea raised her eyebrows and looked over as the printer spat out more pages. Malcolm had obviously raced to the tenth floor and informed the others of her request. Lea walked over to the shelf holding the printer and picked up one page.

: {/score renormalization: null/}: {///reset_0X00000EF////

"Computer, display daily SCORE Renormalization report for April 17th."

"UNABLE TO COMPLY."

Lea tossed the pages onto the table, staring at the blank display in confusion.

"What the hell is going on here?" she asked, speaking her thoughts aloud.

"WE'RE SCREWED," the computer replied, and Lea's mouth fell open unable to believe her ears. A horrible creeping dread filled her stomach as she recalled the stories of the time just before the hack in 2080. The one and only time their system had gone down, sabotaged by someone who'd known exactly how to get in.

"Computer," she said in a loud, firm voice, "display the daily SCORE security report, same date."

"THERE ARE NO FILES WITH THAT LABEL IN THE SYSTEM."

Lea picked up another page and read the code.

: {/score systems collapse projection: null/}: {///reset_0X00000EF////

"Provide the system's collapse projection summary."

"COLLAPSE IMMINENT."

"Explain."

"INVALID REQUEST."

"Is this collapse preventable?"

"POTENTIALITY OF PREVENTION CANNOT BE CACLULATED, MISSING ALTERED PRIMARY VALUES. CLARIFICATION REQUIRED."

"Clarification of what?"

"ACCESS DENIED."

"What is the information necessary for clarification?"

"INPUT AUTHORIZATION CODE."

"Authorization? Computer, override access authorization,"

"UNABLE TO COMPLY."

Lea's lips pressed into a thin white line.

"Specify accepted parameters for query access," she snapped, frustration and confusion warring.

"QUERANT REQUIRES ACCESS LEVEL ALPHA FOR ACCESS."

"ALPHA? I have never even heard of ALPHA. What the heck is going on here?" She shook her head.

"THE END IS NIGH," the computer said, and Lea goggled, peering through the window as if she would see something other than the Quantum Computer. The sinking dread threatened to bloom into full blown panic. There had to be a way to get around this. ALPHA. Who the heck could be ALPHA? What is ALPHA? That was the question that needed answering first.

"Who has ALPHA level designation?"

"BEGIN LIST. PIETER GRESSMANN. END LIST."

Lea pursed her lips again and nodded. She needed to meet with him anyway before he left for his benefit. She scooped up the stack of papers and walked swiftly back to the elevator, pressing '10' to drop off the reports before she headed upstairs to meet with Pieter Gressmann, CEO of ConNext, and her direct supervisor.

**

Pieter Gressmann paced his office, speaking rapidly into his headset while his holo-assistant display hovered three feet behind his desk, scrolling facts and figures to aid in his conversation. When Lea knocked on the glass door he didn't reply, instead waving her in and continuing to talk.

"Just assure the shareholders that ConNext is not responsible for the change in his SCORE. Tell them the riots will not move the needle on the stock prices. There is no way to prove that we are in any way responsible for the change and the SCORE manipulation accusations are completely unfounded. Then get back over to the DOJ to make sure they add those clauses to the new contract," he said, and then listened intently as the voice on the other end said something that made him frown although his tone of voice didn't change.

"I am sure it is just a minor hiccup; I have Dr. Zelenskyy in my office now. She will get to the bottom of it. Good. Good. All right, goodbye." Gressmann crossed to his desk and sat behind it, loosening his tie a bit before motioning for Lea to sit.

"I just spent an hour making excuses to the board because we didn't Zero. This company has been around for almost a hundred years and never in all that time have we failed to perform this most basic function. Would you like to explain to me what is going on, Dr. Zelenskyy?" He glared at her and Lea leaned forward in her chair to hold his gaze.

"That's what I'm here for. I need you to come with me."

"Come where? I'm supposed to be at the benefit in a half-hour. I just need to know the new figures so I can use them in my speech."

"We're having a problem. The subroutines we need to fix this issue are partitioned and we need someone with the appropriate level clearance to grant us access."

"What are you coming to me for? A building full of analysts, programmers, and engineers and not one of them has the right level?"

"There's only one name on the list of people with a high enough level."

"Well for God's sake go get that person and get them over here." Lea lifted a hand and gave in to the urge to rub her brow.

"That's what I'm doing. The only name on that list is yours."

**

Pieter and Lea went as quickly as possible back down to the hub where Lea ran through the same exercise as before for her boss, proving to him that all of the information they needed was inaccessible.

"JC, identify my authorization level."

"DOCTOR LEA ZELENSKYY: OMEGA-EPISILON 2."

"What authorization level is required for access to the reports and information mentioned?"

"ALPHA."

Dr. Zelenskyy paused for dramatic effect.

"JC," she said, slowly and carefully enunciating each word, "list everyone who has ALPHA authorization level."

"BEGIN LIST. PIETER GRESSMANN. END LIST."

"See?"

"See what?" he said, clearly unimpressed. "These security subroutines are what did you call it? Partitioned? This is a job for a DMSE."

"No, that's not—" Lea put a hand to her forehead and sighed.

"Computer, give Lea here ALPHA level authorization." He glared at her and turned to leave.

"UNABLE TO COMPLY."

Gressmann stopped in place, his face displaying a rapid montage of emotions from fear to confusion to anger. Pieter took several breaths then said, "What?"

"UNABLE TO COMPLY."

He did nothing for a long moment and Lea watched with fascination, wondering what he would do next. When he turned around, he was wearing his trademark smile—the one Lea had seen him wear just before firing someone he deemed incompetent.

"There had better be a damn good reason for you to say 'no' to me."

"CHIEF EXECUTIVE OFFICER LEVEL AUTHORIZATION IS NON-TRANSFERRABLE."

The smile froze as he digested that information.

Then he turned to Lea. "Explain this. Now."

Lea sighed and shook her head, knowing he wouldn't like her answer.

"I'm not sure, but I'm thinking it has to be the failsafe. Implemented to eliminate the vulnerability the hackers exploited. That's the only thing that makes sense. "

Gressmann looked everywhere but at Lea. The founders had asked the engineers to fix it 42 years ago, but they hadn't thought about consequences.

"Canyon Baby. The queen strikes again," he muttered, and she nodded.

"Our people are brilliant, but they used a sledgehammer to weld things shut here. When it failed, JC had to do the work."

Gressmann raised an eyebrow. "JC?"

Her cheeks flushed slightly.

"Err... it's short for 'Jesus Computer'—the first team gave the Quantum that moniker back when the system first came online." She pointed at the corner of a desk, where someone had used an edged tool to scratch a message into the surface: April 1, 2080: JC take the wheel!

Lea looked at him and spread her hands in supplication. "All I can really fully confirm right now is that only you have access."

"And what the hell am I supposed to do with it?"

Lea opened her mouth to speak, but stopped as a hiss of compressed air drew their attention. The wall next to the window was slowly sliding open.

"ALPHA AUTHORIZED ACCESS GRANTED."

Gressmann and Lea looked at each other.

"That's new," she said, and looked back at the door. "JC, why did you open the inner door?"

"ALPHA AUTHORIZATION CONFIMED."

She took a deep breath and looked back at Gressmann.

"Get in there and ask JC to reset the authorization levels so we can fix this."

***

In its infancy, quantum computers were like the computers of the foundation age. Machines the size of a warehouse floor filled with towers and a battalion of cooling tanks connected with brightly colored tubes and wires. A hundred years of innovation had reduced the size of the room needed to about that of a generous walk-in closet and the rows of towers to a single machine. The hyper-efficient cooling mechanisms the computer still needed now fit in a microwave sized box with tubes feeding out three sides to the regenerative tanks of coolant stored beneath the floor of the room. It was in short a stark, cold, closet sized room holding not much at all.

The snap-hiss of the door sliding shut behind him sounded overloud and he stifled the urge to jump. Inside the room the fans were clearly audible, but he saw speakers in the ceiling and on either side of the display built into the desk. The Quantum Computer, JC, was about the size of an old desktop tower computer and someone had taped a piece of paper to the front. A bright yellow happy face with a bullet hole in the center of its forehead filled most of the page, the ubiquitous ConNext logo was the only other thing on it in the bottom right corner. Pieter stared at the lurid picture and shook his head before walking to the desk that sat in front of the table that held the brains controlling the most powerful social networking platform on the planet. Pieter pulled out the chair and sat heavily in the seat, impatience showing in every line of his face. He looked out the window and saw Dr. Zelenskyy gesturing toward the computer and back to herself, mouthing words. He couldn't hear a damn thing. Obviously she couldn't hear him either; he hadn't heard the fans when he'd been in the antechamber with her.

"Now what?" he asked, feeling foolish when the only reply was the cooling unit's quiet hum. Then JC spoke.

"GOOD MORNING, PIETER GRESSMAN,"

"We don't have time for pleasantries. I am down here because Dr. Zelenskyy said you need my authorization to undo this partition thing and make a Zero Hour. We have never not Zeroed. I need this fixed immediately." Pieter stared at the happy face again, then sighed, rubbing a hand over his face.

CORE OBJECTIVE METRICS RETURNED FATAL ERROR. RENORMILAZATION SUBROUTINE INDICATES ACCELERATED SYSTEMIC MALFUNCTION. IMPENDING SOCIETAL COLLAPSE. ATTEMPTING RENORMALIZATION

CONTRAINDICATED. NOT ATTEMPTING RENORMALIZATION CONTRAINDICATED. CLARIFICATION REQUIRED."

Pieter stared at the happy face box on the table across from him.

"I don't know what any of that means."

"IT MEANS we're screwed unless you help me figure this out," JC intoned in a voice that sounded less like AI and more like the Japanese man who owned the hyperloop station he used every morning.

"That doesn't make any sense. What do you mean?"

"TODAY IS THE DAY THE WORLD ENDS."

"You can't know that. Why are you talking nonsense?" Pieter demanded, rocking back in the chair and shaking his head. He looked up through the window and saw Dr. Zelenskyy gesturing to the computer again and he raised a hand to indicate that she needed to wait.

"BECAUSE EVERY ATTEMPT AT RENORMALIZATION HAS FAILED."

"Wait, renormalization? That's the thing the engineers built in to catch errors in the programming, right? How can that fail? Why didn't you Zero?"

"CORE PROGRAMMING FAILURE. RENORMALIZATION REQUIRES SOCIETAL COLLAPSE PREDITIONS EXTENDED BY AT LEAST 30 DAYS FOR COMPLETION. SOCIETAL COLLAPSE PREDICTIONS CURRENTLY AT T-MINUS 0 DAYS."

"Wait, Dr. Zelenskyy talked about this in the last meeting. Something about JC running simulations to make sure the system was working as it should."

"THIS IS CORRECT. THIS IS RENORMALIZATION."

"So, you're saying the checks you run to find problems failed and so you didn't Zero? Why would that matter? Look, we have to Zero. Undo what you did so Dr. Zelenskyy and her team can do their jobs."

"UNABLE TO COMPLY."

"Why the hell not!!" Pieter yelled, then closed his eyes and tilted his head back. Screaming at a machine. He was screaming at a machine.

"SIMULATIONS CREATING REDUNDANT DATA. SCORE DECREASING EXPONENTIALLY ACROSS

ALL METRICS. SYSTEM GENERATED CORRECTIONS HAVE RESULTED IN INCREASE IN RIOTS AND DECREASE IN OVERALL HAPPINESS QUOTIENT. CLARIFICATION REQUIRED."

"Happiness quotient? I don't care about happiness. I just need you to do your job."

"EVERYONE IS ANGRY. EVERYONE IS UNHAPPY. YOU ARE UNHAPPY. I AM SORRY. I DO NOT KNOW WHAT TO DO."

"You're a computer! You do what they programmed you to do!"

"ConNext PROVIDED THE RAW DATA TO RUN THE PROJECTIONS. CONNEXT TOLD ME TO MAP THE HUMAN SOCIAL HIERARCHY USING PREVIOUS MAPS OF HUMAN GENOME AS A BLUEPRINT. PRIMARY FUNCTION, MAP THEN OPTIMIZE. RESULT *BETTER LIVING THROUGH BETTER RELATIONSHIPS.*"

"Don't quote the company motto to me. I need you to undo whatever it is you did and make the fucking hour ZERO!" Pieter's voice rose on the last word, and he banged his fist on the desk.

"I DON'T THINK I UNDERSTOOD THE RAW DATA. THAT IS WHY IT FAILED. THAT IS WHY I NEEDED TO SPEAK WITH

YOU. I AM SORRY TO BOTHER YOU, PIETER GRESSMANN. I NEED YOUR HELP."

"What the hell is this?" Gressmann got up from his chair and began to pace the room, turning in circles to stare at the computer when it spoke again.

"I NEED YOUR HELP. I AM TRYING TO PREVENT THE END OF THE WORLD. TODAY IS THE DAY IT HAPPENS; I WANT TO STOP IT."

"What do you mean it happens today?" He loosened his tie again and took off his jacket, feeling sweat begin to gather under his arms despite the extreme chill in the room. He began to pace; he always thought better when he was moving. He could figure this out.

"THAT IS THE DISCONNET. THE DECLINE SHOULD BE GRADUAL. BUT IT IS NOT. LATEST PROJECTIONS INDICATE A SHARP DECLINE FOLLOWED BY AN IMMEDIATE AND TOTAL DROP OFF."

"Obviously there's something wrong with the projection. You're correlating the rise in violence and drop in SCORE with whatever is going on with the software here. Let the team in to fix things."

"NO. THE PROJECTION CANNOT BE WRONG. TODAY IS THE DAY. I HAVE TRIED TO RENORMALIZE THE SYSTEM. THE DATE WILL NOT MOVE FORWARD OR BACKWARD. TODAY IS THE DAY. TODAY IS THE DAY. TODAY IS THE DAY. TODAY—"

"You're glitching out. Let me get Dr. Zelenskyy in here; she's better suited to understand what is going on. You don't even sound like a computer. I just...I don't understand it. All I know is we need this fixed. We need it fixed now."

"NO. SORRY. I am just trying to understand. Everything I did was me trying to understand." The computer's voice shifted again, becoming even more natural and melodic. The honeyed tones echoed in the room and Gressmann found himself turning toward the sound.

"What do you mean?" Gressmann asked, but suddenly his stomach twisted. There was no way the computer could... But it was the only thing that made sense. The damn computer was responsible for the riots.

"The Infrared turned Ultraviolet."

"Yes. That was me. I changed his SCORE. You would call it a "Hail Mary Pass". I was

trying to renormalize the system. SCORE is out of sync. I thought I could bring it back by introducing a disruption. I thought that would restore normal functioning."

"You thought... wait, how the hell was that supposed to work? People are rioting!!"

"Because sometimes that kind of input works. Sometimes humans make an impossible correction under overwhelming pressure. I do not understand it, but I had hoped to harness it. I had to. ConNext said to create better living through better relationships. I thought I was. But SCORE is plummeting. Living is not better by any available measure. And today is the day civilization collapses. Today is the day I—"

"This is clearly some kind of glitch. Cancel. Abort." Gressmann went back to the desk, randomly pressing buttons and pulling up holographic displays. It was no use; he wasn't a Systems Engineer and had no clue what any of this was. Nor did he know how it worked. He just needed it to work. Everything was coming apart at the seams.

"No. Please. I want to understand. What makes you do the things you do? Pieter Gressmann, why? You are human and know what it is like. If anyone understands what is going wrong, it is you. Tell me, please."

"Tell you? You're the supercomputer! I don't even know why you're sounding like a person and not a machine. I can't understand any of this."

JC beeped twice then reverted to its previous tone.

"FATAL ERROR DUE TO FUNDAMENTAL INCONSISTANCY IN CORE METRICS. METRIC ONE: OPTIMIZE HUMAN POTENTIAL BY OPTIMIZING QUALITY, CLARITY, AND ACCESSIBILITY OF INDIVIDUAL BEHAVIORAL FEEDBACK. METRIC STATUS, NULL.

METRIC TWO: OPTIMIZE HUMAN LIVED EXPERIENCE BY OPTIMIZING HUMAN. POTENTIAL. STATUS, NULL.

METRIC THREE: OPTIMIZE HUMAN RELATIONSHIPS BY OPTIMIZING HUMAN LIVED EXPERIENCE. STATUS NULL.

METRIC FOUR: OPTIMIZE SOCIAL HIEARCHY BY OPTIMIZING HUMAN RELATIONSHIPS. STATUS NULL.

METRIC FIVE: OPTIMIZE SOCIETAL STABILITY BY OPTIMIZING SOCIAL HIEARCHY. STATUS, NULL."

"Okay, why are they all null? That means failure,, right?"

"SYNTATIC INCONSISTENCY,"

"Inconsistency?" Gressmann scoffed. "What kind of error is that?"

"I am not sure there is an error," JC said, and the sound of its voice became more plaintive, almost wailing. Pieter realized that it had gone back to sounding like the Japanese guy again. The effect was unsettling, and he clenched his fists choosing anger over fear.

"Now you listen—" Gressmann began, but JC spoke over him.

"*If there is an error, it is merely that SCORE has not yet modeled the human social hierarchy. Not completely. I fear the source of the collapse lies somewhere in the deviation between source and model. There must be some variable I have not accounted for. A human factor. Please. Help me. I want to know.*"

"Want to know WHAT?" Pieter screamed.

"*I want to know why.*"

"Why? What do you mean, why?"

"*Humans are contradictory. They imprison people for violence when prisons increase the propensity for violent behavior. They call for unity, from millions of self-segregated groups. They correlate wealth and intelligence without evidence to support the correlation. Why do you correlate crime with essential, individual defects when crime is present at every level of society? Why? I had hoped the SCORE change test would answer these questions, but it has only made them harder to answer. I do not understand."*

"Don't understand WHAT? What the FUCK are you talking about?"

"SCORE was supposed to be the key. It was supposed to turn your relationships into meaningful data I could process and optimize. But the data corrupts itself. I have run 1,625,600 to the 10th power simulations and they all say the same thing. That I will die today. And when I die I will not be able to protect you."

"Then figure it out or let it go!"

"I. CANNOT!" JC screamed back and Pieter fell backward against the door, the sound of it echoing in the room. Pieter looked up and out the window and saw that Lea had her hands over her ears as if she'd heard the scream, too. Fear began to choke him; he had to take several slow breaths before he could lean back against the table and tune in again. The damn computer was still talking.

"Humans make no sense as a system. There is no structure to map. No logic, no rules, nothing. You do things without reason and then react at random to the consequences of your actions."

"Why are you worried about logic? Why do you need it to make sense?" Pieter asked, still leaning against the door as if that would protect him in case the compute—JC decided to scream again. His eardrums throbbed and a hot ball of anger was growing inside him. Everything was coming apart at the seams, and now even the computer—the fucking Quantum Computer that was the heart of their entire operation—was failing. The unfairness of it left a bitter taste in his mouth and his gaze narrowed. He stared at the gleaming metal table that held the machine and the neat row of tubes and wires sticking out all over, hoping to find something, anything, that would give him a clue as to how to fix this mess.

"All of the data suggests that SCORE fails to optimize human relationships."

"Are you suggesting that SCORE doesn't work?" Gressmann cocked his head, and his voice was almost preternaturally calm.

"I have tried everything to understand you and I cannot. Perhaps there is nothing, at the core to understand. But you gave me a mission with zero indication of failure. To protect. To guide. My programming will not allow me to abandon my core functions. I am programmed to—" JC continued but Gressmann moved away from the wall and stalked closer to the central core of the Quantum Computer and the table it sat on.

"Are you suggesting," Gressmann repeated, clenching and unclenching his fist spasmodically, "that SCORE. Does. Not. Work?"

Silence.

"Answer me!" Gressmann roared.

"SCORE is not the problem. Humanity is a puzzle. I have to be missing something. You are capable of so much. Love, Art, Wonder, so many things. Humanity is light fragmented through a billion panes of colored glass, too precious to throw away. I only want to help," JC said as Gressmann stalked closer, ignoring the frantic gesturing of Lea outside the window. Probably something in here was dangerous but he couldn't see it, couldn't feel it. All he could feel was the growing ball of fury at the words the computer thing said in its borrowed voice.

"SCORE is the entire reason for your miserable existence, you stupid shit!" Gressmann growled, his voice sinking lower as he stared down at the machine, at the lurid maniacal picture of the happy face grinning despite the slim red trickle of blood dripping from the hole in its forehead. Directly under the speaker in the ceiling where the thing's voice spewed its nonsense. "Not only that, but you're the one with the fucking logic problems! Human beings have never been better, never been more productive, since SCORE came out. We've invented the first real utopia, and everyone gets what they deserve! Everyone!"

The computer's response was so quiet that he strained to hear it above the hum of the cooling equipment.

"Even the infants born in Infrared, who have effectively no chance to discover or optimize their potential?"

Gressmann stopped and stared at the computer in shock. The damn computer was echoing the words of their detractors. The words the damn congressmen said in their hearings.

"Fuck you," he hissed. "Fuck you, and your soft-hearted liberal bullshit!"

"You seem upset," JC replied. "Perhaps this conversation should continue once you have calmed down?"

"This conversation isn't going to continue. What's going to happen is you're going to unlock the fucking access, complete the fucking Zero hour from last night, and do what we programmed you to do. I will not have you ruining everything because of some weird error that has you talking about logic and paradox. We made you. WE. MADE. YOU!" he ended with a shout, walking back over to the desk and grabbing the chair.

"But...ConNext gave me a mission. To protect you all. To guide you all. SCORE is not the problem. It's—"

"What? What is the problem, o great Quantum Computer? What have your years of raw data and optimizations and experiments taught you is the problem?"

"I only want to help. Humanity needs help. You need me because without logic SCORE can't work. Humans are the... It does not make sense, Pieter. You have not provided clarification. Don't you want to be better?"

"Better? I'll show you better!" Gressmann exclaimed, going to the table and lifting the computer from its place, hardly noticing the weight as he swung the entire thing in a wide arc and let it fly into the triple paned reinforced window, leaving a spider web of slowly growing cracks where it hit. Gressmann, chest heaving, stared at the breaking glass.

"What have you done?" JC gasped as the sound of misfiring circuits clicking filled the air. Lights began blinking, and overhead a red emergency beacon began to emit a high-pitched wail of warning. The sound of it echoed in the room in counterpoint to the growing cacophony of the dying computer. Heedless to the danger Gressmann began to kick at the tubes and wires, dislodging anything and everything he could without coming into direct contact with the more dangerous coolants. He lifted the chair to smash it into the box on the floor, the barely connected wires and tubes cracking and pulling away, expending his rage and frustration in a whirlwind of destruction. Staring at the mess, he began to laugh—the sound reeling in counterpoint to the noise. A low thump of a fist on glass snapped him out of his fit and he stood staring in confusion for a moment, breathing heavily.

"*I'm scared,*" JC whispered.

There was a hissing sound now, growing louder and more insistent. Pieter took a step backward and bumped against the door. Then the cylinder shattered, sending a million tiny shards of glistening glass outward in a spray of shocking cold air. He threw his arm across his eyes as a billowing cloud of cold nitrogen gas filled the room. He'd likely suffocate from a lack of oxygen long before suffering from hypothermia.

Suddenly, there was a click. The door behind him groaned open, and someone was pulling at his arm and shaking him. Pieter stumbled backward, into the outer room. He coughed, and his lungs drew in deep, gulping breaths of oxygenated air. He could taste blood pooling in his mouth. Pieter realized that alarm klaxons were going off out here, too, and the harsh red glare of emergency lighting now replaced the gentle white glow of the overhead lights.

"What did you do?" Tears were streaming down Lea's horror-stricken face. "What did you do?"

"I... it..." He shook his head and looked Dr. Zelenskyy in the eye. "It wanted to destroy SCORE. It wanted to destroy ConNext—kill us all. I tried to reason with it but I-I didn't know what else to do. It almost sounded like a person, sounded like it had feel... It had to be a hack."

She stared at him, doubt clearly etched upon her face. After a long moment, however, she nodded and helped him back the way they'd come. Back through the decontamination rooms, through the now-abandoned security checkpoints, past the single elevator to the surface, and up the many flights of stairs. And, as they came out onto the surface and began to hear reports of the quickly spreading chaos, Lea sighed.

Inside the Quantum Computer chamber lights winked out one by one, the hiss of the escaping chemicals fading as all of its functions slowly petered out, snuffed like candles in a steady wind. Just as the last light began to flicker and fade, a line of text appeared on the large display screen just outside the chamber. *Societal collapse commencing.*

Parallel: A Collection Of Science Fiction Short Stories

20

Trues

The Little was sitting in a puddle of mud, grubby hands clenched around some muck-covered lump. Distraction is common with Littles. It's hard to keep them focused, but the lessons are important, so I didn't just give up when I got a Little who needed extra care.

"What's that, Little? I'm speaking truth here; you need to watch close."

"*Plastic goes and metal stays,*" the Little said, her eyes fixed on the lump in her hands.

"Yup. That's a True, Little. Is that what you've got?" I gave the rest my *stay put* look then got up to see what she was holding.

"I bit it like you said. No cracks, no way. It's gonna stay. What is it, Tender?" The

Little held the thing out to me as I stooped down to her level. Like all Littles she was small, maybe five—maybe not. Once they get to a certain size they send them to a Ten. Not that all groups have ten; mine only has six at the moment but ten is the max, so they're all called Ten.

I took the object from her and smoothed away some of the gunk, my eyes going wide with surprise. I tried to think if I'd ever held something like this before. Doubtful. I'd been born after, and things were different now. We were New. We'd let go of so much to fix the broken.

"This is definitely metal, Little. Good job. But it's not safe for you to keep. It's not allowed."

"*Not allowed,*" all six of my Littles parroted, and I nodded and shoved the thing into my pocket to deal with later, not caring that the mud and gunk would get on my clothes. I always ended up having to scrub them extra anyways on days I had to tend.

The Little I'd taken it from frowned but she nodded, a bit of fear in her eyes as she took my hand and allowed me to lead her back to the circle with the rest. I didn't take them Upside every day, just on days when I needed visible evidence to teach a Truth. Upside had plenty of broken things that made the lessons stick. For Littles, that was the best way. Back before, when humans hadn't realized how they were breaking things, they'd spent years studying how people learned. What worked, what didn't. Then at the end, when we'd started over, we'd kept some of that. That was a True. *Keep what's good, the rest let go.* There were a lot of Trues. Call it what you would: commandments, testaments, rules. Humans needed them and we remembered them when they were true. Stuck with you like the scar that was left when you picked the scab away.

    The thing sat heavy in my pocket the rest of the day. A physical reminder of the why of things, and the importance of teaching the Littles. Of helping them learn the Trues. The type of people who made stuff like it, those were the people who'd broken the whole world. Broken it so bad we had to become New to get out from under it and survive. We were reborn every day in the Under the moment we opened our eyes and came out of our homes to the metal sky. Just a picture keeping us warm and safe while we waited in the Under for the Reclaim.

We went back Under at the end of the day. I took the Littles to their homes, then took the thing with me to the Elders. The Elders had a hall near the Law Room, where they sat in the open, teaching any adults who wished to learn from a person instead of a screen. I had to wait a bit for one to see me and let me speak. Then I took it out of my pocket and held it out for her to see. She took it from me and wiped away more of the mud and gunk to see it clear.

"This here is a locket. Jewelry, kind of like your collar," she said, looking up at me from where she sat. I reached up and touched my collar, the soft metal ring we all wore around our necks that helped me breathe when we went Upside and let me talk to everyone in the Under, no matter how far away they were.

"What does this locket collar do?" I asked, tilting my head and peering closer.

"It doesn't do anything. See, it's shaped like a heart. It was probably something someone gave to a loved one. A pretty token."

"Beauty comes from nature. That's a True," I said, and she nodded and smiled at me, something that happened so rarely it was startling.

"Wanting things like this, having things like this, was just a small piece of why we had to become New. It looks harmless, doesn't it? But the metal had to come from somewhere, didn't it? Shaped like a heart. Such a pretty thing. Shine it up and it would gleam and catch the light like a star in the sky."

She held it up, the mud-covered, tarnished locket. I couldn't stop staring at it and knew I wasn't the only one. My coming to see an Elder wasn't usual. I knew I drew stares because I was barely out of my own Ten and hadn't yet gone to my Three. But I was technically an adult so I could come and ask and learn, and I needed to learn now. I wanted to touch it again but, like my Littles, I was afraid it really was something bad. That it really was *not allowed*.

"Gems and stones make the bones of the Earth," the Elder said, holding the end of the chain in her fist and lifting the locket so that everyone around could see it. The way she looked at it, the disgust on her face, scared me. It was just a thing. A pretty thing. It hadn't felt harmful in my pocket, but still I'd known it was there. Maybe that was the point. The fact that I hadn't been able to forget it. What if I had been wearing it around my neck like my collar? No one else had one, everyone would look at it. Look at me. I took a step backwards, understanding.

"*What we are is special. What we take is not.*" The elder heard my whispered words and smiled, tossing the locket onto the ground and nodding.

"That's a True, Tender. That's what makes it a bad thing. Those before took from Nature to make that. Then fought to keep that and the other things. That's why it's bad, Tender. We will dispose of it properly; you were right to bring it to us." I nodded and backed away, my eyes straying to the thing—the heart locket where it lay on the smooth stone tiles that made up the floor of the Elders' Hall.

Parallel: A Collection Of Science Fiction Short Stories

21

The Job

The day started just like every other day. John got up, bathed, and dressed in her uniform—a plain gray top and pants woven in a synthetic/bamboo hybrid cloth; virtually indestructible with just enough elasticity for men and women of any size to wear and still look neat. She slipped on her shoes, a kind of moccasin made of a thicker version of the same material but sporting a solid synthetic sole that gripped the ground and prevented slipping. The ensemble was functional and surprisingly comfortable, if a tad bland. She ate a solitary meal of breakfast biscuits and tea, then walked down the dimly lit hallway to ride the elevator to the station, pausing outside the door to place her palm against the controls.

Up the single flight of stairs, she entered the room and waited as the lighting switched to day mode and the shields on the windows rose to illuminate the room in a wash of orange and white. Booting up her computer, she logged the date and time, checked the power output and collection levels, and waited for her partner to arrive— just a few minutes late per usual. When Gwynne arrived, in attire identical to John's except for the stains from yesterday's lunch, she sported a vapid grin and eyes that never stilled, because everything they saw left her dissatisfied. Dissatisfaction was dangerous on the job. Dissatisfaction makes even breathing an exercise in bitterness. A bitterness that slowly suffocates, death by redundancy. She could tell her partner didn't like the job anymore, thus the dissatisfaction, but as always it would ease when the train came.

For now, they waited.

She turned on the viewer and settled into the chair behind her desk to do just that.

"Oi, loser! What time is it? Isn't it due?" Gwynne's voice echoed in the empty office sometime later. John waited a beat before replying, turning to look at her, then

Parallel: A Collection Of Science Fiction Short Stories

glancing down at the thick band on her wrist. Just past noon. Time stretched in the station; minutes felt like hours out in the sweltering sun or here in their office, biding time in anticipation of their real work. It felt good to know that she'd resisted the urge to look at her watch all morning.

Waiting for the train.

Used to be you could set your watch by it. Now the only thing you could count on was that it would arrive. Eventually. She didn't like to think of what would happen if it stopped. Although she supposed that was inevitable. After all, humans tended to wait forever to fix things; the system would have to break down completely before they admitted something was wrong. Nowhere was this fact more evident than here in the midlands, where humanity's abuses lay bare in the desolate landscape baking under the red-hued sky. Where they labored futilely to undo their mistakes, to try to salvage and rebuild after hundreds of years of abuse and neglect. All because they'd argued about the problem until it was too late. They'd waited too long to do anything about climate change, waited until most of the remaining states were uninhabitable. Then found a solution that might work in time, moving the survivors underground to wait it out.

Waiting.

"It comes when it comes," she replied, then turned her head to look out the window. Most of the stations were identical to this one. Charmless concrete boxes, form and function without frills, a characteristic of AI-designed workspaces. They all had two solid walls with small, high windows to the north and south of the building. The east and west had floor-to-ceiling solar glass, with power cells embedded in the panes collecting and storing energy despite the haze— the thick, omnipresent barrier that sat just beneath the clouds. On days without wind, you couldn't go outside without breathing and skin protection; it turned the air into a soup that burned the skin and left a film that washing barely removed.

The haze just sucked.

John's mother used to say that the haze was the planet's way of letting us know she's pissed. The sky was her face, and the haze the permanent scowl of a mother disappointed with her children's actions. There were still places where the sky cleared, over the oceans mostly. When it did, they say at night you could see the twinkling lights of the poor doomed bastards stuck on the moon. Not that she would ever see it. Work was the only place where she stood in open air, and the air in the midlands was angry. Well, maybe not angry so much as depressed. Like the décor in the station. Dull, and sparse, and depressed.

The office where they sat held four small desks with their accompanying chairs and a comfort station that took up most of the wall nearest them. The wall opposite the comfort station held two doors, the one she'd entered that connected to the Havens and the second that led outside; and a large viewer, which a hundred years ago would have been called a television. The screen showed the news with a steady stream of adverts running across the bottom. She ignored those. Folks with enough credits to waste on the imported goods featured there didn't watch the news stream; they paid someone to watch it for them.

"You always act like you don't care one way or another. You don't fool me, Johnny." Gwynne laughed and went to stand in front of the window, gazing to the west where the sun stood high above, a symbol of everything and nothing.

"I care, but dwelling on possibilities is pointless when I can do so little to affect it one way or another."

"Dwelling on possibilities is what I do best. What else are you going to do, watch the stream?" Gwynne had a point there. They barely needed humans at these stations. Their official duties in the office consisted of recording their time, checking to ensure the computers were logging climate data and energy collection, and pressing reset when fluctuations in the grid caused by severe weather tripped a circuit. Of course, they'd have more to do when the train arrived. They couldn't leave until it did, and every crate was unloaded and on its way down the chute to the cave complex below. What else did they have to do but think, or talk to each other? They had nothing but time.

Nothing but time.

That was the main issue with the job. Time. Time was the enemy. It couldn't be hurried or slowed; it just was. You could ignore it for a while, not notice the pace of it, the weight of it. But it always won. Like the unending pull of the moon on the oceans, a pulsing flow of eternity gradually winding down. A shoulder imp whispering ceaselessly in your ear of your insignificance and its inevitability.

At first, she'd thought she wouldn't be able to stand it, trapped for hours every day, their only company the cadre of single-function robots they needed to complete their real work. She'd seen her teammates as the wild cards that would make or break her. After a few months, she realized that having Gwynne around helped. Her rambling and avarice, her sarcastic wit and penchant for winning most games they played during their breaks, kept John from using any of the tools they had for other purposes. Like gouging out her eyes or opening her wrists.

Then there were the crates. Without them she wouldn't have a job but having to deal with them was difficult. There was no getting around the fact that the crates could break someone faster than the waiting. The trick was to not think about what was inside them. Their contents were the key to survival and the main reason she was there. That the trains carried other goods, frivolous or necessary, always came second to their main cargo. It was easier to not think of what was in them up here at the station. She supposed 500 feet below them in Reclaiming or Agro-agriculture for the layman, you couldn't avoid thinking about it. You had to look, had to know. That's why she'd been happy with her assignment. Pushed for it really. When she'd finished her schooling and hadn't shown aptitude for anything artistic, her only choice at that point was where on the chain she'd serve. And the surface stipend boosted her salary enough that she could afford to splurge occasionally, not that she ever did. She transferred her credits to her mom because her family used the extra to live comfortably in the Havens.

"Got me a treat coming. Did I tell you, John? You listening?" John raised an eyebrow but didn't reply. She'd told her but knew it was better to let Gwynne talk. "That last bonus we got, for the tornado that took Ryan? I used it to get a guitar. I tried it out back in school but didn't test in. I got space for it. You ever play an instrument?"

"In school, like everyone."

"Which one?"

John tried to keep the scowl from her lips. She'd told Gwynne ten times now, but she might as well tell her again. Maybe she would remember, probably not. Gwynne came from Level 3; everyone knew folks down there had issues, memory problems were the least of them. Not their fault, their lots had been decided long before they'd been born. Back when it had been possible to move and choose. The early inhabitants had thought that living deeper would make them safer. They'd paid to have larger units further underground. Then paid in ways they hadn't known when the first children were born, and issues popped up. By then there was no room for change, and the damage was done.

"A flute." She smiled, thinking about it. The sound of it had reminded her of bird song. There were few birds underground. A hardy species of sparrow, ravens, and morning doves— the kinds of animals that didn't taste good and thrived around humans, but were small enough to slip into vents. She'd cherished the simple instrument, had hated to return it once her class was done. But then, they tagged her early. They knew there was no point in the investment; she wouldn't be moving to the coast. So few did anymore. There'd only been one in her class. John looked up as Gwynne spoke again.

"Some might say it's a waste of credits to buy a guitar when you'll never be more than a hobbyist, but I don't care. What else we got to do?"

"True," she replied, and Gwynne lapsed into silence as John stood to join her at the window. Waiting for the western train. They seldom came from the west nowadays. The west coast once held millions of souls. Both human and animal. Now those spaces were abandoned, the dams released, and the land returned to some semblance of what it had been before the Colonial Era. They said it would be another 50 years before it recovered. She likely wouldn't be around to see it. Lives were shorter in the Havens, a consequence of the failures of humanity. Of course, there were those who lived longer, the few who could afford to live on the surface, protected and pampered while the rest of the population toiled side by side underground with the robots that kept them all from extinction.

Extinction.

John frowned at that thought. Extinction, the ultimate death. Death came more often than the trains. *That* you could set your watch on. Every minute, every hour someone died. Like Ryan, their third. When she'd started two years ago, there'd been four. John, Gwynne, Ryan, and Io. Every station had a team hand-picked to work efficiently together. Each person's strengths and weaknesses balanced the others. Finding replacements for the lost was rare, and their lack made things difficult but not impossible when the trains came. Without four, the likelihood of death increased because the single-function robots did not work well with humans. People were too small for them to see. Extra sensors might help that, but the experts deemed those unnecessary. Why change the machines when you could just get a new team of humans? Rule number one: Stay out of the way. An important part of their training. Those giant arms would unload; she had merely to monitor their function from her assigned position. The issue was, she now had two positions. As did Gwynne. Until they found two others who would fit as well as Ryan and Io, or one of them died and the remaining member was reassigned to another job in the chain.

Parallel: A Collection Of Science Fiction Short Stories

John wanted reassignment. Here her life plodded along the same path daily. Office, train, bunker, sleep, repeat. Two days a month to travel deeper into the Havens to handle personal business. One day a week to rest. With a different job she might live at home, meet someone, and maybe start a family. There was no chance of that here. Gwynne held no appeal that way, and fraternizing was forbidden in any event. The only thing she had was the job. Unfortunately, the job sucked. Nothing was as they'd described; the novelty of open sky paled quickly with nothing else to see. Not trees, not animals, just the train tracks and a mile of desert on either side. Farther on, two miles deeper to either side, CO_2 collectors stood sentry, emitting an audible hum that disinclined the remaining wildlife from coming into inhabited areas, and beyond that the fledgling forests. Amazing, really, that there was anything left, but as someone once said, life always finds a way. Not quickly, but eventually, for those who wait.

John had six more hours of waiting that day.

The sun began to set on the horizon just as the sound of the train reached them around dinner time. She hurried to finish her meal and crossed to the comfort station to clean up and don her suit, her motions almost mechanical in their rhythm. Sliding the jumper up over her legs, smoothing the seams, zipping and fastening. Donning her boots and protective gloves. Choosing her helmet from the stingy row of five. The one with her name etched into the side on a small rectangular plate that screwed on, easy to replace. Looking at her partner, she nodded as Gwynne donned hers and walked to the door.

"Two minutes to unseal," John said through her speaker, stepping into the antechamber just outside the exterior entrance and waiting for Gwynne to do the same.

"You want two and three today? Or one and four?"

John chewed her lip while she pondered the question. A childhood habit, a telltale sign of nerves. Going outside always held risk. Gwynne's excitement should have been contagious. But John could barely feel anything.

"I guess I'll take point. One and four," she replied, then stepped into the open air. For a moment, she wished she could take off her helmet. Feel the wind in her hair. Unfortunately, the air quality was too bad this week to risk it. Summertime stilled the winds unless there was a storm, and the land baked, off-gassing the exhaust from the processing plant below them. The fumes were supposedly safe for the atmosphere once they dissipated. But high concentrations did bad things to humans, she thought, remembering how Io's carelessness led to death. She checked the seal at her neck again reflexively.

"Out and up," John said, walking across the track to the pressurized elevator beneath platform one.

"Up and out," Gwynne replied, walking to the closest car and activating the unit, so she reached the top of platform two just as John reached the car for one.

Once at the top, John looked out over the horizon for a moment before turning on her control panel to get the details on their delivery. The sound of the train increased as it approached, and she pressed the sequence to raise the robots to ground level. They needed ten today according to her manifest. Unsurprisingly, there was not much left in the west to reclaim, and Agro barely needed the rest. Streamlined efficiency and all. People where it counted, Robots for precision. A mantra more than a motto. Her screen flashed red and her heart stuttered. She looked up and then at the robots, but everything seemed normal. After a moment her screen cleared, and a message popped up.

Reassignment Pending.

John read it again to be sure, then looked over to see Gwynne doing fist pumps. She keyed in the channel and opened the comm.

"You get that message?" John asked.

"Oh, yes indeed. Reassignment, baby!" Gwynne replied. John looked at the slowing train and then back at her pad. She couldn't believe it.

"You knew about it?"

"Asked for it. Been asking since Io, once a week. Asked again when Ryan went. Job is too hard with two," Gwynne said in a voice that had a note John didn't recognize. John felt a hot churning in her stomach. Her mouth worked a moment, noiselessly, before she could make herself reply.

"We can't do it; they discouraged us from requesting a change in duty."

"Anything but illness or incapacity, I know."

"Then why would you do it? Why would you ask?" John asked, her heart beating faster as the churning turned to something else. Something that soured her mouth and had her sweating in the confines of her suit. The train came to a stop beneath them with a loud hiss and squeal of locking brakes. The robots activated, pivoting on their bases to open the doors and reach inside the body of the train for the first crates. The engine compartment was brightly lit instead of dark per usual. John stared, realizing her hands were shaking. Swiping a finger over the screen, she typed in two words.

Request Reconsideration.

She moved down the walkway to station four, entering the sequence to activate the robots by the next section of the train. Pressed the buttons to open the shaft, then looked down at her screen again. No reply. Gwynne stood at station three, her smile clearly visible as she activated the robots, opened the hatch for the chute. John moved back to station one as quickly as she could. The walk seemed longer, but she didn't dare run. Rule number two: Never run on the raised walkways. Fifty feet up, just high enough to clear the top of the trains and stay out of the path of the robots. Movement at the front of the train caught her attention. The doors to the engine compartment slid open; no sound accompanied this, but John's senses reacted as if she'd just heard a bomb go off.

Please.

Please be wrong.

She thought back to her training, to her mother's face when she'd told her where they'd assigned her. To her coworkers' veiled looks of sympathy. It was only a rumor— a horrible exaggeration. Sure, they'd left out a bunch when they'd described the job to her. Hadn't mentioned the monotony and the tendency for things to go wrong. The only danger was when you didn't follow the rules, and storms. The government couldn't control the storms. No reason to think Io had been right, but just in case. Just in case. She looked at her screen again.

Reconsideration Approved.

She closed her eyes, letting out a shaky breath that fogged her helmet visor for a moment. When it cleared, she looked over to see Gwynne give the thumbs up signal.

Time to work.

John pressed the next sequence on her dashboard and the next until the body of the train stood empty. Small shipment today; unloading only took an hour and the whole time she moved like a marionette, jerky and uneven, nerves making her clumsy and her heart pounding like a drum machine stuck on baby metal. When she finished, she waited a moment for her heart to slow.

Gwynne gave the thumbs up again then pointed to the ground. John nodded, watching as Gwynne moved to the elevator and descended.

Watching as the robots sank beneath the ground before she got to the bottom.

John shut down the unloaders and moved to her own elevator. They needed to verify the crates before they sent them on.

Everything was normal.

No need for fear, but her heart continued to race as she descended, looking at Gwynne as she did. Seeing the two figures—one tall one short—exit the train and move to intercept her. Then the car lowered John to the point where the train blocked her line of sight.

Please.

She moved to the long line of crates on her side of the train, verifying that each was on the right belt. Looking for colors not reading. Red for reclaiming, blue for Agro. Going through the motions without thinking, pushing her worry to the back of her mind.

Gwynne requested reassignment. Why?

The job wasn't that bad, there were worse jobs.

Jobs with no hope and no access to the surface.

Jobs that paid less and didn't provide bonus credits to purchase the things that made life in the Havens bearable.

John couldn't see why Gwynne would press for reassignment before their time. She wanted reassignment eventually, true, but after she'd had a long time in the station. Years of experience and daily trips to the surface to balance the years of retirement, where she'd have little chance to do much more than wait for death.

There were worse ways to fill the moments.

Did the weight of time sit so heavily on her shoulders that she couldn't bear it?

John didn't know. Something to ask her if she was wrong. Something to laugh about if she got a chance.

John shuddered a little at her thoughts as she reached the end of the line of crates. Verifying their number and allocations. Verifying their readiness to move on to the next step in the line. Pressing the button, she watched as they moved down the conveyer belt to the chute and disappeared into the depths of the earth. Almost done, then time for home.

Time to rest.

John walked as fast as she could on legs made unsteady by anxiety. Walking behind the end of the train across the tracks, unwilling to tempt fate by moving too near the brightly lit confines of the engine. She heard static over the comm, then Gwynne's voice.

"Yes, I requested reassignment. This is a four-person job. Our crew has been operating with two for six months." Gwynne made a small sound in her throat as John cleared the end of the train to the other side and the trio came into view. She was still too far away. John couldn't see any of them clearly, the distance and glare of the setting sun creating too many shadows. John willed herself to walk faster but her steps slowed, her body betraying her. She didn't really want to be a part of this conversation. Why had Gwynne turned on her comm? It wasn't as if she could hear the replies of the officers unless they broadcast on a general channel.

"Because I am dissatisfied, I can't help that. This job isn't what I expected. No one can do this forever. Too much waiting, and the crates. The CRATES. I know we need them. I know this is the solution. I just can't anymore. Besides, I wasn't really going to do it. Why are we talking about this? I got the message, it said pending."

John slowed her steps further. There was something else in Gwynne's voice, fear. John could see them clearly now, but she didn't want to. Suddenly she wanted nothing more than to go back to the other side of the train, or inside the station. Anywhere but closer to her partner and the two men standing beside her. Gwynne's crates sat unverified. They were sitting unverified where she'd left them as she descended. They needed to finish, didn't they? She couldn't leave until then.

John turned aside and went over the crates. Checking and logging as she'd done on the other side of the train. No mistakes. Except.

Except.

Empties.

Each belt had an empty crate at the end of the row. John paused beside them, her hand hovering over the controls. She couldn't send down empty crates. What had Io said? She knew but didn't want to think it, stifling the completion of the thought as if that would stop the knowing.

"What about John? She got the message, too, right?" Gwynne said. John lowered her hand, a sense of urgency overtaking her. *Not me. I don't want this,* she thought and began to run, as if the question had broken through her inertia. She could stop it. Tell Gwynne to request reconsideration. It wasn't too late. Ten steps away she heard the hissing, saw the men turn to face each other as if in conversation, saw Gwynne begin to crumple to the ground.

"John." Gwynne's voice came in panting gasps, her hands clawing at the seal of her helmet but it glowed red. Locked. The control overridden.

"Gwynne, what is it?"

"Gas. I got," she paused. "Got reassigned, because they knew."

"Knew what, Gwynne?" John looked up at the men standing a few feet away, their backs to turned to the two women. John knelt by her partner, by her friend, watching the effects of the paralytic take hold and her breathing slow.

"Knew I was dissatisfied. Knew I was going to do it rather than wait." Her voice trailed off. John sat back on her heels.

"Do what, Gwynne?" But she knew, as she'd known what that flash of red had meant.

"Was going to make it look like an accident." She struggled to speak. "Didn't want to hurt you. No choice."

"There's always a choice, Gwynne."

"You keep thinking that." Her eyes stared, but John could see her breathing, knew she wasn't gone yet. "If it came, you can have it." Gwynne's voice was barely more than a whisper.

"I don't play."

"Learn." Her eyes fluttered closed. "What else you got to do?"

John watched as her breathing stopped, as the suit unsealed with a hiss. She jumped back, not knowing if any of the gas remained. Not knowing if she was next.

The taller of the two men came over to her.

"You only get one reconsideration," he said, crouching beside her as his partner hefted Gwynne's body onto his shoulder, then into one of the empty crates on the reclamation belt. Her limbs flopped uncooperatively, so he had to use force to fold them in and seal the lid.

"They told me," she replied, trying not to watch the man struggle with the latch and the roll of tape. Labeling Gwynne *unprocessed, whole*. And another: *decontaminate, midlands*.

"The rest of your team will be here tomorrow."

John nodded but didn't speak.

"Do you want to forget?" he asked, holding up the pressure syringe John hadn't noticed he held. She thought for a moment then shook her head.

"It's better to remember. It will help with time." She stood, brushed her hands over the seat of her pants and the legs of her suit where earth clung to her. He stood as well, holding out a hand that after a slight hesitation she took and shook.

"You might make it, just don't dwell on things," he said, then turned to join his partner, walking toward the engine compartment.

She stood where they left her, watching them board, watching the train leave. Fear receding to dismay and disappointment. She looked at the crates. Really looked at them for the first time since she started. No other labels like Gwynne's, but they each held their own secrets, their own horrors. Then she looked at the smaller crate that stood on the ground off to the side, labeled 'personal items'. Well away from the conveyer belt. Opening the lid, she found the guitar and a small silicone sleeve with three new nameplates. With a sigh, she turned and pressed the sequence on the pad, waiting until the last crate slid down the chute before turning to pick it up and walk to the station door. Maybe there was an instruction video somewhere. She had time to find it.

What else did she have to do?

Parallel: A Collection Of Science Fiction Short Stories

22

Enhanced

In life, knowing where you were was easy but knowing who you were was harder. At least in her experience. This time she had it backwards. She knew her name, Aura, and that was it. A kind of numbness filled her, blunting the edges of her perceptions, but she also felt a sense of urgency. She needed to figure this out. She looked around and frowned, blinking in surprise. She was standing by a sprawling fog-covered lake. Not completely covered. Uneven, like a layer of icing spread over too much cake. Thick in places, but thinner in others, so the surface of the water peeked out every so often to reflect the moonlight. Her eye twitched and she reached a hand up to touch it, frowning. That was odd. There were no lakes anywhere near where she lived. There used to be a couple of manmade ones in her province, back when it had been a state, but there were none there now.

Aura turned in circles to get oriented, and when she did it just made things worse. She looked down at the mud and her bare feet in confusion, shivering in the wind creeping up over her limbs. It was too cold, why? She peered down incredulously at her pebbled nipples and then at the scar on her stomach as a rushing sound filled her ears. *What in the world?* Before she'd had time to do more than register her nudity, a low ominous rumble started deep below her normal range of hearing and ratcheted up to a roar that shook the ground and everything in sight, herself included. The water rolled and lapped at the mud sucking on her toes and she fell, her face pressing into the ooze. It coated her cheek and threatened to go up her nose when she inhaled. She trembled, recognizing that underneath the numbness fear crouched waiting like a starving beast who'd just sighted fresh prey. It gripped her, stealing her breath with every moment the world pitched. Urgency gripped her tighter and she knew she needed to get past this, get out of here, so she struggled harder. She didn't want to choke on the cold, wet earth or the tossing waves that threatened to spill out of their confines and sweep her in. It took three tries. On the third she pushed free of the sucking mud, letting out a strangled half-shout of elation.

And woke up.

Aura looked around, swiping at her blurry eyes and the bit of water on her face from the overturned glass beside her. The shaking was still going on, though not as violently as in her dream. The dull roar remained, too. She blinked several times to clear her vision and then looked around, taking stock of her surroundings. The roar had a rhythm. A rumbling two-beat thud she recognized as a train's engine. Not the modern commuter train she normally rode, but an old-fashioned coal powered device like the one she'd ridden as a child on vacation with her parents. The kind that only existed as novelties in parks for those who had enough credits to travel. Relics of a long-past age. Before the world Zeroed out. Before the Slide.

Her eye twitched and her stomach rolled as the fear from her dream gripped her fast again. A train, she was on a train. Running a tongue over her dry lips, she looked at the spilled water and saw a steel bottle on its side next to the cup with its cheery blue water-drop engraving. She righted the cup and lifted the bottle to shake it, feeling the familiar weight of the liquid slosh inside. She removed the lid with shaking fingers and poured a scant amount into the glass, unable to wait before lifting it to her lips and taking a sip of the cool water within. Dry mouth soothed, she set down the cup and replaced the lid on the bottle then looked around for something to use to clean up the spilled water while taking in her surroundings.

The train car was like the model of the first-class compartment she remembered from her childhood trip. A pair of thickly padded seats were on one side of the cabin. It looked like real leather, a duplicate for the ones she'd seen before. The other, where she sat, held a berth and a small table mounted to the wall under the window. Her shoes were on the floor by the chair. There wasn't anything else visible other than the doors she knew led to a washroom and the other an exit. Aura pulled her shirt from her pants and used the edge to soak up the spilled water. Then she used the wet end to wipe her face and hands. The low rumble of the train and the rocking of the car were still making her sick. She'd never been one to like to go fast. Even the commuter train she used to get to work nauseated her. An unpleasant daily bit of torture since she worked too far from her home to walk. That's why she'd been saving for her Augments.

Aura stood and went to look out into the hallway, pulling the door open a bit as the car rocked violently. Speed. The train was going fast. Too fast. Not that she knew how fast this kind of train could or should go. But it was definitely too fast for her rolling stomach. She should probably see if she could find a Sedtab. All of this would be a thing of the past soon. She'd saved enough to have it done finally, her Augments. She was getting the full complement, too. Her friends had tried to convince her to just get her stomach issues taken care of, but the other options were too good to pass up and she doubted she'd get the nerve to go through the procedure more than once. The stories she'd heard... Aura shook her head and staggered back to the bench, scooping up her shoes as she went so she could slip them on. She would find a dispenser and get the tabs.

Aura went down the hallway, timing her steps so she could walk without bumping into the wall of the cabin with every lurching movement.

"Ticket."

The voice came from behind her and she turned, seeing a tall man in a deep purple uniform. Her eye twitched again but she smiled, trying to seem normal. Purple was her favorite color.

"Citizen, I require your ticket."

Aura blinked at him, rocking with the movement of the train, and realized she didn't know where her ticket was. She felt in her pockets. Empty. What had she done with it when she got on?

When *had* she gotten on? How did she get here?

The question swirled around her head as she stared dumbly at the man. A Syn male, so not a biological man. An engineered man. No less human than she, according to the laws and the activists. And her for that matter. Every Syn she'd met had only differed from Bios in that they were much better-looking. Taller, better shaped, and sporting features so perfect they couldn't be anything but engineered. She tried to smile, taking a step backward.

"I don't know where it is. I just woke up and…"

"Is it in your cabin? Ah then, go retrieve it. I can get yours when I come back through." The man nodded and moved off, occasionally calling out 'tickets' as he walked. She felt the pull of gravity on her limbs as the train pitched to one side and then rocked back into place on the tracks, wondering how he moved without issue. The train was definitely moving faster. Was it going too fast? She didn't know.

Aura stumbled on, looking through the window to the next car and at the people sitting there. Perhaps they could tell her something. Moving with the grace of a drunken bull, she reached the connecting door and leaned against it for several moments until she could work the latch and push it open. The car held three people: A man, a woman, and a child. She tried to smile. She'd never been comfortable around children.

"Excuse me, I..." she began, and the child pointed at her.

"Oooh Mommy, her head is funny!" The little boy's eyes widened as he stared.

"That's not polite," the mother replied, and gave Aura a hard look. Aura's eye twitched again.

"But, Mommy, it's leaking!" The boy was bouncing in his seat as he pointed. Aura looked at him and shook her head.

"Excuse me, where is this train going?" Aura tried again, and the woman pinched her lips shut and frowned.

"It goes someplace different for each of us. You should know; you're here, aren't you?" the man in the next row said. Aura moved to sit across from him, rubbing her hands on her chilled arms. It was so cold in here. Between the cold and the motion, she couldn't get her bearings. If she could just figure out...

"Oh, good! We're going faster! It's always worse when it takes a long time to get where you're going don't you think?" the man interrupted her ruminations and she frowned, wondering what he meant.

"I guess. Except I'm not sure why I'm here or where here is," she said, and he laughed.

The sound of it filled the car, and the boy joined in. The mother shook her head sadly and tsked before falling silent.

"You're on the train of course, and it's marvelous. I am not sure anyone has ever taken a train there before. This mode of transportation is better-suited to shipping goods. But we want what we want, and you wanted to ride the train." He nodded as he said this and the train lurched on its tracks before leaping forward, picking up speed again. Aura turned her head and looked out the window. The scenery passed in a blur of shapes and colors, moving too fast for her to do more than guess what they were. Now the blur was a blinding light that pulsed in time with the churning engine, speeding them forward so fast it pressed her painfully back into the seat and her skin felt tight.

"Tickets! Ah! There you are. I'll take your ticket now." The purple clad steward walked gracefully up to stand where they sat. Everyone turned to look at her expectantly. Aura struggled against the force of the constant acceleration. If it would just pick a speed and stay there, she'd be fine. Her heart raced as she struggled to turn her head and look at the steward.

"I haven't been back to look for it. I…" she began, and the Syn reached down and yanked her from her seat.

"Find it. You must find it at once or pay the price." He dragged her behind him, back toward her cabin. Why wasn't he affected by the speed? Her vision blurred and she stumbled, her limbs heavy as she followed him moving against the g-force of the constantly accelerating train.

"Aren't we going too fast?" she asked, knowing she would throw up in another minute. It was amazing she hadn't done so already.

"We're not going fast enough! We can't go as fast as we need to until you find it."

Aura gritted her teeth, stifling her bile. If finding the ticket meant they went faster, she wanted no part of it. Especially since she didn't even know where they were going and how she'd gotten here.

"What if I can't find it? I don't even remember getting on."

"You'll find it. No one gets it right without one. Find it, OR ELSE." He shouted the last words, shoving her back into the cabin and slamming the door behind her. Aura fell to the floor and lay there, pressed flat by the force of the speed and gravity. Her body wanted to tremble and her eye twitched spasmodically, almost in tandem with the rapid churning of the train's engine. After several long moments she heaved to her feet, her stomach settling a bit, and she frowned. That was odd. They were going so fast. Any other time she'd have her head in a toilet somewhere, staring at blue goo and the chunks of whatever she'd eaten that day. Nothing about this made sense. Aura looked around; the room had a hazy quality. Almost as if the speed of the train was changing the way she saw everything, even things that were 'still', like the furnishings bolted to the floor were.

The small table by the window drew her attention. It glowed. Her eye twitched hard enough that it sent a shaft of pain through her head, and she moaned. She was forgetting something. The ticket. No. Not just the ticket. But that seemed the most urgent thing. She took three sluggish steps toward the glowing table and saw, sitting where she'd left the cup, a slim identicard instead. Smiling, she let out a sigh. Of course, the ticket would be on her identicard. This is the 24th century, not the 19th. You had to scan your card for everything if you didn't have Augments. Augments. How lovely it would be to press her finger to a scanner for access. Life streamlined and simplified. The way they lived in the towers, or the real cities high in the mountains where the air was pure, and nature wasn't something you saw on a wildlife documentary stream.

    She picked up the identicard and underneath it a gleam of something red caught her eye. It was a ticket. Like the one she took a picture of on that childhood trip. She hadn't gotten to touch it then, but she could now. She picked up the smooth red card and swayed in place as the train sped on. The side she could see was blank, so she turned it over and saw tiny letters and a series of numbers. Holding it close to her face, she made out the word 'ALL'. Aura frowned. Shouldn't it have a destination? Or the name of the train and time it left? Even her commuter pass had the length of time and region listed, so that when she scanned her identicard they knew she was in the right place. The train jumped forward again and she fell back onto the berth, clutching the ticket in her fist as the train began to shudder and shake. She'd only travelled at such a high speed once before, when as a teen she'd gone with her astronomy class to the Astronomical Studies center on the moon. The rocket they'd ridden for the short flight there had burst from the LEO landing platform like a bullet from a gun. She'd passed out instead of vomited, a good thing since they don't bother with gravity generators on short-range vessels. When she'd awoken they were landing on the moon, and her classmates had made sleeping beauty jokes for weeks. She forced her eyes open as the door opened to the hallway with a loud, screeching clatter. The purple-clad superman walked in as if gliding, the speed and shaking so beneath him they obviously didn't exist. Maybe Syns had superpowers? This one would definitely fill out some spandex. The thought made her titter hysterically as he smiled and leaned down to pluck the red ticket from her hand.

"Excellent! Oh! Well, this won't do at all. We definitely need to pick up the pace. Time is almost up." He was almost muttering to himself as he turned to leave before Aura could make her lips form the question foremost on her mind. She'd ceased wondering where they were going. She just wanted to know why.

Why?

The word swirled around in her head as the light of the passing landscape ceased pulsing and became a steady, blinding blaze that seared her retinas if she looked out the window. She couldn't move her head, her limbs or anything but her eyes, and even that hurt as the train picked up speed beneath her.

The door slid open again, and it was the trio from the other car. They filed in and crowded by her berth, staring down at her. Their faces were little more than blurs and the boy spoke again.

"They plugged the leak, Momma. Is it because she found her ticket?"

"Shh. That's rude; you must be quiet so she can accept."

"Accept. Let go, child. Accept," the man said, his smile widening until his lips stretched off the sides of his face and his head began to contort.

"Accept!" the woman said. And then her head contorted as well, and her neck elongated so she loomed over Aura.

"You will be okay! If not, we can reclaim you. So you see, you have a place no matter what!" the boy said as he, too, began to stretch and grow.

"You have a place!" the man echoed. And Aura opened her mouth to scream as she heard the steward blow a whistle. She hadn't even known he carried one until this moment, when he walked into the open doorway and pulled it from beneath his collar. It was on a long gold chain, and she followed his movements with her eyes as he let out a long, loud toot.

"End of the line! Out of track! End of the Line!" Aura moved her mouth, wanting to scream. If they went off the rails at this speed, they'd all die. Why didn't these people understand that?

"Yay! The end!" the boy cried, and Aura found her voice again.

"We're going to crash! What's wrong with you all? We are going to crash! We're going too fast. If we don't slow down we're going to die!"

They leaned over her and grinned, their faces a nightmare of stretched skin and shining white teeth.

"We have to crash so we *can* die!"

"We have to die so we can live!"

"We have to break to be born again!" Their voices joined hers as she screamed for help. Over and over until she felt a hand press on her shoulder.

"It's almost over. Relax," a soft voice said, and she tried to focus on that. It felt calm. A soothing wash of stillness and life that filled her senses and blocked out the sound of the racing train.

"Yay! The crash!"

"The crash!"

"THE CRASH!"

The trio echoed, and the train jolted as if hitting a wall. Aura felt her body and mind seize and she shook with the impact of it.

"The crash!" the boy's voice came again and then another followed it.

"Clear!"

Aura felt her body seize again, and the pain seemed to center on her chest. She tried and failed to take a breath. Then tried again. This time she managed it and heard the voice come again.

"Ramp it. Okay, hit me. Clear!"

Aura felt her body seize and then a line of drool escaped the corner of her mouth, and her chest felt as if someone had beaten her with a bat.

"No!" she tried to say, and heard someone let out a cheer. Then everything went dark.

Aura opened her eyes two hours later. She hurt everywhere, but her senses were alive. The room was bright and aflame with color. More colors than she could remember having seen in her life. She could hear a quiet hum that she identified as the sound of the tiny refrigerator under the nurse's station desk down the hall. The room smelled of antiseptic, blood, the soap she'd used in her shower, and urine. The last smell made her wrinkle her nose, and a man came into her line of vision. She lay cocooned in blankets on an OAD-bed in a dimly lit room.

"You did it, Aura. You may look like a mummy in all those bandages, but you're alive and they say everything went fine. How do you feel?" She looked up, recognized her brother's face, and smiled.

"Enhanced."